POPPY'S PLACE

POPPY'S PLACE

•

Sylvia Renfro

AVALON BOOKS
NEW YORK

PRINTED IN THE UNITED STATES OF AMERICA
ON ACID-FREE PAPER
BY HADDON CRAFTSMEN, BLOOMSBURG, PENNSYLVANIA

For my awesome family:
Butch, Lili, and Charlie.

Chapter One

Poppy Sullivan brushed aside the guilty feelings that worried her like a cloud of mosquitos. It certainly wasn't the first time she'd returned late from her travels in the East Mojave National Preserve. Aunt El wouldn't even start worrying until . . .

"Is that a car, Rover?" The question, addressed to her ancient four-wheel-drive vehicle, received the expected response. Years of exploring the preserve's desert highways had made Rover an old, if somewhat uncommunicative, friend.

Poppy squinted into the twilight. A jeep appeared in a sandy wash about a half mile ahead. Its nose pointed toward Hole in the Wall; both doors gaped open. She gasped as she drew closer. Sprawled at full length beside the vehicle was the body of a large man.

1

In seconds she guided Rover into the wash. The figure before her was clearer now. His denim- and khaki-clad body lay at a right angle to the jeep, head resting against a blown-out front tire. An Australian bush hat hid his features.

Poppy pulled on the emergency brake and jumped out of the car. She sprinted toward the prone figure, then stopped dead in her tracks when she saw the sun-bronzed hand move. It caught the hat's brim and tilted it back.

Poppy found herself staring into the most incredible eyes she'd ever seen; amber and fringed by long dark lashes. Eyes that held an unmistakable glint of mischief.

"I thought you'd never get here," he drawled.

Poppy stood frozen in disbelief. Conflicting emotions raced through her. Here she was, in the middle of nowhere, lured out of her car by a man playing dead. She knew she ought to be frightened, but somehow she wasn't. She was too angry to be frightened.

"Very funny," she snapped. "I thought you'd been snake bit or had a heart attack."

"Nope," the man said, slowly uncoiling his long frame from the desert floor. "I haven't seen a snake all afternoon and except for being broken a few times, my heart is just fine."

Even through the haze of anger, Poppy's brain registered that here was an extraordinarily good-looking man. *I'll bet if there's any heart breaking going on, he's the one doing it*, she thought.

While she stood there searching for a suitably devastating reply, Josh O'Donnell took his sweet time dusting off his legs and rear.

You've gone too far this time, Josho old boy, he thought. He'd seen the cloud of dust she'd raised a mile down the road, but he'd expected one of the rangers he'd become friendly with during the last couple of weeks. Instead, the dust cloud had produced a little wildcat who looked like she'd love to chew him to bits.

He gave his knees one last swipe, then rose to his full six feet, enjoying the view on the way up. From the looks of her, that could be one deliciously excruciating end.

Josh smiled apologetically as he surveyed the woman. She was angry, all right. Her cheeks glowed pinker than the desert sunset. She was breathing fast and her blue eyes flashed. Even her hair looked stormy. It had escaped from some kind of clip and swirled around her face in the evening breeze.

Josh thought he had never seen such an appealing, exciting, and *angry* woman. "Listen, I don't make a habit out of scaring young women. I'm awfully sorry."

"Your apology's a little late, mister, and so am I." Poppy turned and stalked back toward her car.

"Wait!" Josh called. "Let me explain."

Poppy was in no mood for explanations. Brad would be driving down this road in less than hour to have dinner with her and Aunt El. If he didn't spot the jeep on his way to Providence, all the better. A couple of hours alone in the desert would give Mr. Golden Eyes a chance to reflect on his foolishness. Maybe he'd think twice before he pulled that trick on anyone else.

As Poppy put the key in the ignition, she couldn't resist stealing one more glance at the stranger. He made no move to approach the car, but for a moment she was held by the intensity of his gaze. In the glow of her headlights, she thought she saw amusement in his eyes, and something else as well. A glint of determination. Somewhere deep in her feminine consciousness, she knew this man wouldn't back down from a challenge.

She turned the key and shifted into reverse. The old car rumbled sluggishly to life as she backed down the sandy wash.

Within seconds, the engine sputtered and died.

"Come on, Rover. Don't do this to me." She turned the key again, and the engine sprang briefly to life. On the third try, it refused to even turn over.

Poppy rested her forehead on the steering wheel. She had progressed barely thirty feet down the wash.

She couldn't believe this was happening. She'd had a new fuel pump put in less than a month ago. She'd take just a minute to collect herself, then put one of the railroad flares she always carried out by the road. She cringed inwardly at the thought of facing that faker again.

Poppy took a deep breath and looked up at the spot where she'd left him. Her gaze encountered no one. At that moment, a deep voice resonated alarmingly close to her ear.

"Lady, you make one hell of an exit."

He opened the car door and stood back, a half-smile curving his lips. "Listen, I don't blame you for being angry. If you'll just let me explain . . ."

"Right now, I'm more interested in getting help than listening to your lame excuses," Poppy snapped.

She hopped down and headed to the back of the jeep for flares and a flashlight. As she did, she saw headlights rounding the curve in the highway.

"Hey, Brad! Brad!" she yelled, waving her arms wildly as she sprinted toward the road. She had no time to light a flare or search for a flashlight. Her shoulders sagged as the ranger's car sped by. *He has all the windows rolled up, the radio blaring, and his mind on Aunt El's cooking*, she thought.

Her stomach rumbled. Dang, she was hungry. Hungry and cold and stuck out in the middle of the desert with some joker who thought he could charm the scales off a horned toad.

Poppy hugged herself. It had been a mild, sunny day but desert temperatures could drop fifty degrees during a twenty-four hour period. She picked her way carefully over the darkening landscape as she trudged back to the car.

"Someone you know?" The stranger stood right where she'd left him, his left hand resting easily against the open car door.

"That, for your information, was our ride out of here. You could have helped me catch him," she bit out through teeth clenched to keep them from chattering. The brightly embroidered cotton blouse she'd put on that morning offered little protection against the cool night air.

"You didn't stand a chance. The car was moving fast and you were much too far away. I don't suppose you have a cell phone?"

"If I had one, you can bet I wouldn't be standing here chatting." She thought longingly of the phone she'd forgotten on her bedside table. "How about you? Did you bring a phone or a spare tire?

"No to both questions. My phone is dead and unfortunately, that *is* the spare tire." The stranger nodded toward his disabled jeep with an infuriating half-smile. He actually seemed to be enjoying the situation. "Come on. As long as we're stuck here, we might as well make the best of it. I started gathering firewood earlier. There should be enough to heat some cocoa."

Poppy was tempted to tell him what he could do with his firewood and cocoa but thought better of it. She contented herself with glaring at him before she jerked the tailgate open.

"I'll never forgive you for this, Rover," she muttered as she rummaged around in the back. Good, her old flashlight was still there, together with the new one she'd purchased a couple of months ago. She switched both on to make sure the batteries were working, then tossed one to her unwelcome companion.

They walked back to his jeep in silence, their footsteps crunching over loose rocks and gravel. Twin flashlight beams danced and played in front on them, darting and dodging over the scrub brush and boulders, connecting, then quickly springing apart.

Wrapped in a Pendleton wool shirt, Poppy sat before a roaring fire, sipping hot chocolate and munching cheese and crackers. She felt deliciously warm inside and out.

The owner of the shirt appeared periodically in the circle of firelight with a load of wood. He was gathering enough fuel to last for hours.

Let him work, she thought. A little penance would do him good. Although now that she was warm and fed, she couldn't summon the antagonism she'd felt earlier.

Finally satisfied with his efforts, the golden-eyed stranger stretched out beside the fire, cup of hot chocolate in hand. "So, are you ready to hear my lame excuses now?"

Poppy couldn't help smiling. He had plenty of moxie, no doubt about that. Besides, she always loved a tall tale. "Go ahead, tell me the story you tell so well."

The stranger answered with a smile of his own. He propped himself on one elbow and began.

"Once upon a time there was a nice young knight by

the name of Sir Josh O'Donnell, who found himself in a very unpleasant situation. He'd spent the last two weeks slaying dragons in the East Mojave, eating pork and beans and shaving out of his coffee cup. Finally, on Friday night, he turned his trusty steed toward the village, hoping for a little refreshment and a hot bath."

He paused for effect.

"But alas, it was not to be. His steed threw a shoe and poor Sir Josh was left without a mount, alone, cold, and friendless."

Another dramatic pause.

"But wait, in the distance, a mighty cloud of dust appeared. Such a cloud could only have been raised by one of the rangers who patrolled this land.

"Now, Sir Josh had met these rangers in his travels and decided to have a little manly fun with one of them. So he pulled his helmet over his eyes and fell to the ground, as if the very breath of life had been sucked out of him.

"Imagine his surprise when he lifted his helmet and saw, not one of the sturdy lads he'd jested with, but the fairest maid in all the land. A maid whose glance pierced his heart more surely than the sharpest lance.

"Sir Josh shared his meager provisions with the maid and wrapped her in his best cloak, but, alas, she continued to look daggers at him. Finally, when it seemed that all his efforts were in vain, she favored him with a smile."

Poppy applauded. "Well done, Sir Josh. I can see you're no stranger to campfire stories."

"Does this mean you've forgiven me?" Josh asked.

"Not even the most hard-hearted of maids could resist your blarney. O'Donnell is an Irish name, isn't it?"

"It is indeed. But you haven't told me your name."

"It's Poppy. Poppy Sullivan."

"And what brings you out into the wilderness, Miss Poppy Sullivan?"

In the flickering firelight, Poppy considered the handsome face before her. If he'd been shaving out of his coffee cup, he'd evidently given up the effort days ago. Thick, sable hair curled around his ears and his eyes gleamed with a primitive golden light. At this moment those eyes regarded her with a look that was . . . hungry.

What would it be like to run her fingers through his hair she wondered. To feel the rasp of his beard against her cheek, his warm lips pressed against hers?

She tore her gaze away from the stranger's hypnotic eyes. *Get a grip, Poppy.* She hardly knew this man. They were stuck out in the middle of nowhere and she was fantasizing about him, for goodness' sake. Her face grew warmer as she wondered if he had guessed her thoughts. It was time to get this encounter on a more comfortable footing.

"So, Mr. O'Donnell, how long have you been in the East Mojave?" she inquired in what she hoped was a steady voice.

Josh laughed. "A little too long, I think."

She tried again. "Do you travel often?"

"It seems like I've spent most of my life traveling. I'm what you might call a rolling stone. But enough about me. You still haven't answered my question."

Poppy looked at him blankly. So much had raced through her brain in the last few minutes that she couldn't for the life of her remember what the question had been.

"What you're doing out here?"

"Oh, I was up at the ranger station at Hole in the Wall. My friend Brad is one of the rangers there. That was his car I was chasing.

"He'll be coming back to look for me soon," she added. She hadn't intended to tell him help was on the way. But with the turn this evening was taking, it might be best to throw a little reality onto the situation. There *was* life beyond the magic circle of their campfire.

"A business or social call?" he asked, fixing her with a steady gaze.

Poppy looked down at her empty cocoa cup, at the fire, out toward the highway, anywhere but into his eyes. Part of her couldn't wait for Brad's headlights to appear, but another, more elemental part enjoyed the exciting, unsettling feelings this stranger stirred in her.

"A little of both," she said quickly. "I went out there to put up a poster and ended up staying longer than I intended."

"What kind of poster?" Josh asked.

"It's a poster I'm distributing for the Friends of the Desert Tortoise. We're trying to educate visitors to the East Mojave that tortoises are an endangered species. Federal law prohibits anyone from collecting, harassing, or injuring them in any way."

"Its hard to believe anyone would hurt a tortoise."

"Usually, it's not so much a question of cruelty as ignorance. People pick the tortoises up because they think they're cute. They take them home and don't have a clue about how to care for them."

Poppy forgot her embarrassment as she continued. "Then there are the people who wouldn't dream of harming animals but don't think twice about destroying their environment. Just last spring, we had a movie company out here who treated the desert like it was their personal sandbox. They threw trash all over, trampled the vegetation, and scared wildlife for miles around."

Josh poked the fire with a mesquite stick, sending a shower of sparks into the night. "That's terrible."

"It gets worse. Some of the crew rode dirt bikes and three-wheelers all over known tortoise habitats. The tortoises were just starting to come out of hibernation. I hate to think how many of their burrows may have been crushed."

"Where were the rangers while all this was going on?"

"There's one ranger for every five hundred thousand acres out here. They caught a couple of the guys and slapped them with fines. If you ask me, they should have tossed them in jail and thrown away the key. People who have no respect for the land and wildlife have no business being here," Poppy said.

Josh sat quietly for a minute as he considered his dilemma. Should he tell this fiery young woman why he had come to the national preserve? Or keep his mouth shut and save a memorable evening?

He might never see Poppy again, he realized with a pang of regret. It was a part of his nomad's life that he had never quite gotten used to. He'd met a few special women in his travels with Outback Productions. Some he'd kept in touch with for a period of time. But his lifestyle didn't encourage lasting relationships. He had a feeling this woman would want and need much more than he had to offer.

Josh studied Poppy through the gently wafting smoke of the fire. She was lovely, no doubt about that. She had the kind of vibrant, natural beauty no amount of cosmetics could impart. But what drew him to her most strongly was the vulnerability he sensed beneath her feisty exterior. She stirred a strange mix of feelings in him. One minute he longed to crush that provocative little body against his. The next he wanted to comfort and protect her.

It's a dangerous brew, Josh decided, *and one I have no business tasting*. Still, he hated to ruin the evening.

As Josh wrestled with his conscience, a pair of powerful headlights cut through the darkness. The Park Service truck had turned into the wash before either of them noticed it.

"Looks like Ranger Brad to the rescue," Josh said, rising to his feet.

Poppy felt as deflated as the jeep's front tire. The fascinating stranger she'd shared a campfire with would soon be going back to wherever he came from. He'd sounded so relieved when he spotted Brad's headlights. Maybe she'd bored him with her talk about desert tortoises. Maybe the strong attraction she'd felt between them was an illusion of the East Mojave twilight. Or, more likely, the product of her overactive imagination.

"Josh, are you holding this woman against her will?" Brad Baldwin asked. At six-foot-two and over two hundred pounds, the ranger could have presented a menacing figure were it not for his joking tone. He looked surprised to see the two of them together.

"It's tempting. But I think I'd be a fool to try," Josh replied with a grin.

Now it was Poppy's turn to be surprised. "You two know each other?" she asked.

Josh spoke up quickly. "This is one of the sturdy lads I told you about. I was expecting him to come to my rescue when you showed up instead."

"Josho is a regular out here. He has a way of turning up when you least expect him. Like now," Brad said. "Say, aren't you ever going to start shooting?"

"Shooting?" Poppy asked. "Shooting what?" Hunting season was over. Brad knew that. What on earth was he talking about?

"Josh's production company is going to shoot a

movie in the preserve," Brad explained. "At least that's what he tells us."

Production company? Movie? It took a minute for the words to sink in. Josh had seemed so sympathetic when she told him how the last movie company had trashed the area. Apparently that was all just part of his routine. And she had fallen for it. Again.

"He certainly didn't tell me." She took off Josh's jacket and shoved it at him. "That's some act you have, Mr. O'Donnell. I should have known you were from Hollywood."

"Van Nuys," Josh said.

"What?" She was caught off guard for a moment by the softness of his reply.

"I'm from Van Nuys."

Poppy just glared at him. She couldn't believe she was having this conversation. The man had no decency. First he tricked her into stopping to help him. Then he led her to believe he sympathized with her concern for the East Mojave. He was lower than a rattlesnake. She was just about to tell him so when Brad broke in.

"I'm not sure what's going on here, but maybe we'd better get it straightened out in the car. Poppy, your Aunt Ella is fit to be tied."

"There's nothing to straighten out." She brushed past Josh and climbed into the waiting truck.

Wedged between the two big men in the front seat of the pickup, Poppy stared straight ahead, trying her best to ignore the pressure of Josh's leg against hers. She answered Brad's questions succinctly. It seemed to be the fuel pump again, and yes, she really needed a new car. Then she lapsed into a stony silence.

The thirty-minute ride to Providence felt like thirty hours. Finally, Brad brought the pickup to a stop in front of the combination store, restaurant, and two-pump gas station that served as the town's social center. A hand-painted wooden sign over the door read "Poppy's Place."

Poppy could see lights on in the living quarters attached to the back of the store. Aunt El was probably worrying herself sick, thanks to Mr. Josh O'Donnell. She would have been home long ago if he hadn't tricked her into stopping.

"Thanks for the ride, Brad. I'll call the tow truck in Amboy tomorrow." She fidgeted impatiently as Josh took his time about opening the door. When he finally let her out, she strode across the parking lot without a backward glance.

"So you're the Poppy on the sign?" Josh called. It was half question, half statement.

Poppy turned with her hand on the front door. "That's right, Mr. O'Donnell," she said sweetly. "There's one store and gas station in a fifty-mile radius, and I own it." The door slammed behind her.

Josh let out a soft whistle and climbed back into the truck.

"Come on, old buddy. You can bunk with me tonight," Brad offered. He couldn't resist ribbing his friend a little as they headed back to Hole in the Wall. "You really know how to charm the ladies, Josh old boy. What did you say to make her so mad?"

"It wasn't what I said so much as what I didn't say." Josh gave him an abbreviated version of what had happened.

"Wow, I don't blame her for being mad. Come to think of it, if I wasn't such a nice guy, I'd be mad at you too. I was really looking forward to that home-cooked dinner at Aunt El's." Brad rubbed his ample midsection regretfully.

"Poppy's aunt is a good cook?"

"The best. I've been cadging dinner invitations from Poppy ever since I was knee-high to a red ant."

Josh sat up, interested. This was his chance to find out more about the mercurial Poppy Sullivan. Somehow, he had to get back into her good graces. It definitely would not be in the company's best interest to create more hard feelings among the locals. Also, he had to admit, she was an intriguing woman.

"You two must have known each other a long time," he probed carefully.

The jovial ranger didn't need much encouragement to open up. "I met Poppy when we were both ten years old. Believe it or not, I was a skinny, asthmatic kid. My parents moved to the desert for my health.

"Poppy and I got acquainted on the school bus to Needles. All the kids from Providence stuck together.

One day a couple of playground bullies started picking on me. Poppy tackled one of them and wrestled him to the ground. He was twice her size, but she sat on him and twisted his arm until he said he was sorry.

"The other guy was so shocked to see a girl beating up on his buddy he didn't know what to do. He just stood there with his mouth hanging open. It was really something."

After all the years, the admiration in Brad's voice was still evident. Josh found himself wondering if they had ever been more than friends. If not, it certainly hadn't been due to a lack of interest on Brad's part.

"Has Poppy always lived in Providence?" he asked.

"No, she moved here about two years before I did, when Ella and Mike Sullivan adopted her. She doesn't talk about her life before she came here. I don't know, maybe she doesn't remember much. She was pretty young. Mike died a few years ago. Since then Poppy has run the store."

Josh sat for a minute and digested this information. "What kinds of things do they sell?"

"Groceries, a few household items, soft drinks, the usual mom-and-pop kind of stuff. Poppy put in a section of trail supplies that she's pretty proud of. We get a lot more campers and hikers around here since the government made it a national preserve.

"Then, there's the restaurant part of the business," he continued. "Aunt El does the cooking. They have the best hamburgers, homemade chili and corn bread, a different kind of soup every day in the winter, plus a blue plate special. Top it all off with a piece of El's pie and you've got a meal fit for a king."

Brad groaned. "Man, why'd you have to get me on that subject?"

"Sorry," Josh said with a grin. He could feel more sympathy for his friend if he wasn't so pleased by what he'd heard. Maybe, just maybe, he'd found a way to make his best interests and Poppy's one and the same. He'd have that little wildcat eating out of his hand yet.

Chapter Two

Poppy looked up in surprise at the firm knock on the door. She'd just started coffee and opened up the cash register in preparation for the day's business. The store wouldn't open for another hour.

"See who it is, Poppy," Aunt El called from the kitchen. The smell of baking apples and cinnamon perfumed the air as her pies bubbled and turned golden in the oven.

Whoever it is, he must need a caffeine fix pretty bad to be out this early on a Monday morning, Poppy thought.

A blast of cold air hit her when she opened the door. Hardly less welcome than the freezing draft was the man who stood on the front porch stamping his feet and blowing into his hands. Josh O'Donnell, trying his best to look pitiful, and doing a darned poor job of it.

"What do you want?" Poppy asked.

"Ah, if you could but spare a crust of bread and a place by your fire. I'm afraid I might freeze if I stand out here much longer."

Lord, thought Poppy, *he never gives up*. She'd have welcomed anyone else on such an inhospitable morning. But this particular snake oil salesman could peddle his wares elsewhere. She certainly wasn't going to fall for his line again.

"The store opens at 8 AM, Mr. O'Donnell. I suggest you come back then." She ignored a twinge of guilt as she shut the door in his face. Let him sit in his jeep and run the heater, she thought. He's not going to get frostbite in the Mojave Desert. Although it would serve him right if he did.

Josh knocked again.

"Poppy, for goodness' sake, who is that?" Aunt El came around from the kitchen, drying her hands on a dish towel.

"Some jackass looking for a place to bray."

"Penelope Sullivan! I'm surprised at you." Aunt El couldn't suppress a smile as she bustled past Poppy to answer the door.

"Can I help you?" she asked.

"Morning, ma'am," Josh said. "I'm sorry to trouble you so early but I saw your lights. I wonder if you might have a cup of coffee for a poor, cold traveler?"

Aunt El chuckled. "'Tis little enough you ask," she said. "Come in and welcome."

This, thought Josh, could be the start of a beautiful relationship. Now, if only he could win over El's lovely niece.

Inside, Josh looked around the spacious room, divided into three sections. To his left stood several round tables covered with red checked cloths. A long L-shaped counter wrapped around the surprisingly large, professional kitchen.

To the right was a small but well-stocked grocery store. Josh noticed a cold case with milk, butter, cheese, lunch meat, and soda pop. Next to it stood a freezer, and in the right-hand corner of the store was a section labeled "Trail Supplies." Several video games blinked and hummed through a partially open door in back.

Picture windows facing the Providence Mountains were shuttered this morning against the cold. A venerable pot-bellied stove, set against the far wall of the dining area, gave the room a glow of warmth and domesticity.

Presiding over this cozy scene at the apex of the counter stood Poppy Sullivan. Her lovely face reflected a mixture of defiance and chagrin. Like a kid who knows she's behaving badly but is not about to admit it, Josh thought.

"Sit right here, Mr. . . . ?" Aunt El motioned to the wooden chair closest to the stove.

"Josh O'Donnell, ma'am."

"Ah, an Irishman. I knew it," said Aunt El. "Sit and warm yourself. I have to check my pies. Poppy, are you going to ask Mr. O'Donnell what he wants?"

Josh tried hard to keep a straight face. Years in the field had taught him the importance of establishing friendly relations with the locals. Judging from Poppy's expression, he had a long campaign ahead of him. He couldn't help enjoying this minor victory.

Poppy slammed the cash register shut and marched across the room, indignation radiating from her little frame. Energy seemed to ripple from the ground up through the ends of her curly brown hair.

She had her hair pulled back again, more tightly this time. Even so, it seemed to be straining against whatever held it in place. Josh had the feeling it might escape and come tumbling down around her shoulders at any moment.

"What *do* you want?" Poppy asked.

Now there's a loaded question, thought Josh. There were many things a man might want of Poppy. For right now, he'd settle for a little conversation.

"A few minutes of your time," Josh answered. "I'd like to apologize for the other night. I should have told you I was scouting locations for the nature documentary my production company will be shooting in the national preserve. I didn't know if I'd ever see you again, and given your strong opinions about movie companies, well, I didn't speak up soon enough. If you could join me for a cup of coffee, I'd like to explain how Outback Productions works."

"I'm sorry, Mr. O'Donnell. I'm busy. Do you want to place an order?" She shot him an accusing look before shifting her gaze to a point just above his head. Her right foot tapped the tile floor as she awaited his reply.

Josh glanced around at the empty cafe. "Ah. Well, in that case, I'll take a piece of whatever is producing that wonderful smell. And a cup of coffee. I'll be back this way tonight," he added. "Maybe we can talk later."

Poppy had already headed toward the kitchen. "I'll be busy then too," she called over her shoulder.

I can wait, Josh thought, *I can wait.*

"What's the capital of California?"

The school bus had just come in from Needles, discharging its usual assortment of children. Poppy looked up from the canned goods she was stacking on a shelf in the grocery section.

Ashley Evans' big brown eyes regarded her expectantly. Her third-grade social studies book and lined notebook papers were scattered across the counter.

"That would be Sacramento. Aren't you a little young to be studying state capitals? I remember helping your brother with his state report when he was in fifth grade."

"It's extra credit," Ashley explained. "Mrs. Wilson says we should know more about the state we live in."

"Mrs. Wilson is right." Poppy cast a glance toward the game room in back of the grocery store. Ashley's brother Rodney and cousin Eldon were battling dinosaurs on the vintage video game. The rest of the kids had already been picked up by their parents or relatives.

"Where's your mom today?" Poppy asked.

"She had a doctor's appointment. We might be getting a new brother or sister."

Poppy gave the child a hug. "That's wonderful, sweetie."

Ashley shrugged. "I guess."

"Let me know if you need any more help." She couldn't blame Ashley for being unimpressed. New brothers, sisters, and cousins were regular occurrences in the Evans clan. She mentally ticked off the number of children in Ashley's branch of the family. Was it six or seven? No matter. The Evanses were sure doing their part to populate the East Mojave.

The school bus overflowed with second- and third-generation Evans children, plus quite a few others who were unrelated. They frequently stopped by after school to buy a treat, play video games, or start their homework if their parents were late picking them up.

Other than the kids, only one customer had come in this afternoon. Homer Bell. Poppy stifled a smile as she looked at the dapper little gentleman. A retired academic, he'd come to the desert to indulge his love for reading and research. Rumor had it he was writing a scholarly dissertation about the American Southwest.

Poppy didn't need any dissertation to tell her his main interest was in Ella Sullivan.

She crossed to the table where Homer sat sipping coffee, reading a newspaper, and casting an occasional furtive glance at Aunt El. She couldn't help feeling sorry for the little guy. He was kind of cute in his tweed jacket with the leather elbow patches.

"Would you like more coffee, Mr. Bell? Or another piece of pie?" She held a coffeepot at the ready while Homer checked his watch. He always stayed precisely one hour, no more, no less. Poppy wondered what could possibly hold him to such a rigid schedule.

"Yes, I think I have time for another cup. Would you like to join me?" He peered over the top of his reading glasses and gave her a shy smile.

Poppy looked around the cafe and store. Ashley's head was bent over her papers, her lips pursed in concentration. The boys seemed intent on their video game.

Her gaze rested on Aunt El, who bustled around the kitchen. El looked much busier than normal for this time of the afternoon. The high color in her cheeks betrayed her awareness of Homer's presence.

Why not? Poppy thought. A sly smile touched her lips. "I'd love to join you for a cup of coffee. Do you mind if I ask Aunt El, too?"

A look of sheer panic darted across Homer's face. "Oh no. I mean, I'm sure she has things to do," he stammered.

"Nonsense. Aunt El works much too hard. She needs to take a break now and then."

Poppy saw a ray of hope light Homer's gray-green eyes. He self-consciously smoothed the wavy salt-and-pepper hair that fell onto his forehead. "Well, all right. If you're sure it's no bother."

"Not at all. I'll just go get her." She turned, leaving Homer to tug at his shirt sleeves and square his shoulders.

Aunt El sat at the long butcher block island in the center of the kitchen, methodically wrapping napkins around silverware. Her back was to the dining room.

"Aunt El?"

Ella jumped. "Goodness, child! You startled me."

"What were you thinking about?" Poppy caught the guilty look on Aunt El's face. Honestly, the two of them were worse than a couple of high school kids. "Never mind. I've come to extend an invitation, from Mr. Homer Bell, to join him for a cup of coffee."

Aunt El's complexion went from rosy to pale in seconds. "Oh, I couldn't," she whispered.

Aware that Homer was watching them, Poppy sat down next to Aunt El and picked up some utensils and a napkin. "Why not?" she asked. "He seems like a nice man."

"I know. It's just, I feel so strange. Mike is the only man I ever loved. I'm too old to start keeping company with someone else."

Poppy smiled at the old-fashioned expression.

"Uncle Mike's been gone for two years now. I know he'd want you to be happy. What harm would it do to give the man a chance? Who knows? You might become friends."

Aunt El placed both hands on her hips. "Aren't you a fine one to talk, now? 'Give the man a chance,' she says. That nice young Josh O'Donnell has practically done back flips to make up with you, but you're too stubborn to give him the time of day." By the time she finished her speech, Aunt El's cheeks were bright pink again.

"That's different," Poppy protested.

"Oh? And how is it different?"

"Josh O'Donnell is a scoundrel and flim-flam man. He's no better than the last filmmakers who came out here and trashed the national preserve. If he had honorable intentions, he wouldn't have hidden the fact that he was making a movie. Nor would he have tricked me into stopping to help him."

The sound of the cafe door closing cut off Aunt El's reply. As they argued, Homer Bell had quietly let himself out. The two women watched as his shiny late-model Ford sedan retreated down Providence Road.

Aunt El rose and looked after him. "Oh, dear. Now I've hurt his feelings," she said.

Poppy put her arm around her adopted mother's shoulders. "He'll be back. You can make it up to him with a piece of pie. He loves your pie."

"I hope you're right." El's worried expression indicated that she was far from convinced.

"Poppy?"

Poppy turned to find Ashley looking at them with enormous brown eyes. She'd completely forgotten about the child.

"Who's Josh O'Donnell?" Ashley asked. "And what's a flim-flam man?"

"Never mind, sweetie," Poppy said. "Just do your homework."

For the next two weeks, Josh was a frequent visitor to Poppy's Place. He came in almost every morning to eat a leisurely breakfast and swap stories with the miners, ranchers, and retired folk who were the cafe's regular customers.

During the day, he explored the preserve. When he returned late in the evening, Aunt El saved him a blue plate special. Josh took a bite, then tried to outdo his previous night's praise. Aunt El always declared him full of blarney but she clearly enjoyed their nightly ritual.

It seemed everyone was talking about the nature documentary Josh's production company would soon begin filming. Only Poppy remained aloof.

As always, she had a kind word, a smile, or a joke for everyone who entered the cafe. Everyone but Josh. With him, she put on her most professional manner. He could charm the socks off the rest of Providence but she knew exactly what he was up to. She had never seen such a blatant public relations campaign.

Poppy gave one of the tables a swipe with her towel.

It certainly didn't help that he was Irish. She knew Aunt El missed Uncle Mike terribly. So did she. But that was all the more reason not to be taken in by this . . . this charlatan.

To give the devil his due, Poppy had to admit Josh had been good for business. The cold weather didn't bring many hikers but the locals practically fell all over each other to sit and talk with him. Poppy's Place had sold as many breakfasts during the last two weeks as they usually did during the peak seasons of spring and fall. She'd even had to get a rancher's wife to help out.

Poppy studied Josh and Aunt El for a long moment. They seemed deeper in conversation than usual. Periodically, one or the other would glance in her direction, then quickly look away. Something was up. She wished she knew what.

She took one last look around the dining room. Everything was tidied from the lunch rush, which had consisted of Josh and a couple of tourists off old Route 66. Things should be pretty quiet now until the school bus comes in from Needles, she thought.

"I'm going out back, Aunt El. Holler if you need me."

Poppy walked the length of the yard to the last patch of winter sunlight. She sat on a wooden bench and leaned against the side of the house, her face to the sun. She'd always loved their backyard. It had a secluded, private feeling, even though the business was just steps away.

Tucked into the L formed by the store and house, the

yard caught the morning sun but was mostly shaded by late afternoon. Grape trellises along the south-facing fence were bare now. In the summer they formed a cool green barrier between her retreat and the gravel parking lot.

Poppy dug her hands deeper into the pockets of her warm jacket. Directly in front of her, in the northeast corner of the yard, were four long, narrow mounds of dirt. *Valentino, Clara, Lillian, and Myrna. All tucked in for their long winter's nap.*

"A penny for your thoughts."

The deep masculine voice made her jump. She hadn't heard Josh come out the back door. He stood on the steps watching her.

It seemed that no part of her life was safe from Josh's intrusion. He ate in the cafe morning and night. He parked his motor home across the street. Now he'd invaded her private sanctuary. She wouldn't get any peace until she talked to him. Besides, she was darned curious about the whispered conversation she'd just witnessed in the dining room.

"I was thinking about my tortoises."

"Tortoises? What tortoises?" Josh asked.

"They hibernate this time of year." She pointed to the long earthen berms. "Here. In their burrows."

Josh walked slowly out into the yard. "Four burrows must mean four tortoises. Where'd you get them?"

"I'm the adoption officer for the Friends of the Desert Tortoise. I take care of tortoises that have been injured or removed from the wild until good homes can be found for them."

"I've read a little about desert tortoises," said Josh. "Once they've been taken away from the desert they can never go back again, can they?"

"I'm afraid not. Tortoises are very territorial creatures. Each has a home range with two or three burrows and a good seasonal supply of water and vegetation. When they're removed from their range, they become disoriented and often die of starvation or exposure.

"Once a tortoise has been in captivity, for even a few days, there's a danger of exposing other wild tortoises to a severe respiratory infection. The infection is quite common among pet turtles and tortoises and can be treated with antibiotics. But it's been known to wipe out whole populations in the wild."

"Once the last individual of a race of living things breathes no more another heaven and earth must pass . . ." Josh quoted.

"Before such a one can be seen again," Poppy finished for him. "William Beebe. I'm surprised *you're* familiar with him."

"There's a lot about me that may surprise you. What do you call your little friends?" Josh sat beside her on the bench.

Poppy caught a whiff of leather from the battered jacket Josh wore, mixed with the fresh, outdoorsy scent of a young, healthy male. The warmth of his body tempted her on this cold February afternoon. For a moment she had an insane impulse to snuggle closer and inhale more deeply his intoxicating scent. Instead, she shifted farther away. "The male is Valentino. The females are Clara, Lillian, and Myrna."

"The sheik and his harem. And would they be named for Clara Bow, Lillian Gish, and Myrna Loy?"

"Aunt El has a passion for old movies. I was raised on everything from the silents through Hollywood's Golden Era in the thirties and forties. We have VCRs, even in Providence."

"So the girl who hates Hollywood cut her teeth on it." A lopsided smile tugged at Josh's mouth.

Poppy knew when she was cornered. "All right. I admit it. Like everybody else, I was a little starstruck. Having a feature film shot in the national preserve was pretty exciting for all of us. I let myself be taken in by a bunch of smooth-talking Hollywood hypocrites." She paused and looked Josh straight in the eye. "But it won't happen again. And now, maybe you can answer a question for me. Just what have you and Aunt El been cooking up?"

"Ah, I can see you're a woman who comes right to the point." As Josh turned toward her, the late afternoon sun illuminated flecks of brown and green in the depths of his golden eyes.

A person could drown in those eyes. The thought popped unbidden into her brain. Why did he have to be so darned attractive? She gave herself a mental shake and paid attention to what Josh was saying.

"I've made your aunt a business proposition, to which she's tentatively agreed. With your approval, of course. You may have heard that I'm going to start shooting my documentary next week."

"I heard," Poppy said. In fact, she'd heard about little else since Josh made their store the unofficial headquarters of Outback Productions.

"I'll be working in the preserve with a camera assistant and a sound technician for six to eight weeks. I need to supply at least two full meals on site. Aunt El has offered to cater breakfast and lunch if you're willing to deliver the food to us. You'll be well compensated."

Poppy stared at him for a moment as the audacity of his proposal sunk in. Knowing how she felt about the last movie company in the East Mojave, it had taken a lot of guts for him to approach her.

"Where are you all planning to live?" she asked.

"In two motor homes that we'll park as close as possible to the locations. I've arranged for all the necessary permits and cleared the campsites with the Park Service."

Poppy thought for a minute. Suddenly Josh's crazy idea began to make more sense. If she drove out to the location every day, she could make darned sure he honored his commitment to treat the preserve with respect.

"And how much would this compensation be?" she asked cautiously.

"At the outrageous rate currently charged by catering companies, and added to the amount your aunt says you've saved, it should just about pay for a replacement for Rover."

Poppy struggled to retain her composure. She'd been trying for months to save enough for a new vehicle. One thing or another always came up. Now Josh was offering her the opportunity to keep his production company honest and maybe earn a new four-wheeler in the bargain.

"Mr. O'Donnell," she said, extending her hand, "you've got yourself a deal."

Chapter Three

Poppy stood by Rover's rear cargo area, checking off the supplies she and Aunt El had collected for their first day in the catering business.

"Let's see, two ice chests. One for cold food and drinks, the other for hot dishes. Three thermoses filled with coffee, two with vegetable soup. Enough camp dishes and cutlery to serve a small army. Plenty of sodas. Two big coolers full of water. Napkins, dishtowels, soap, plastic tub, table cloths . . . and a partridge in a pear tree."

Aunt El chuckled as she straightened up. She'd just finished loading the last hot container into an insulated chest. "I know it seems like a lot, but working out in the fresh air surely gives a body an appetite. Be off with you now. You don't want to be late your first day on the job."

Poppy backed into the campground at Hole in the Wall at precisely 8 AM, one hour before Josh had requested that she serve breakfast. Two motor homes were parked in the gravel parking lot but all was quiet within. Late risers, Poppy thought, even for city folk.

Volcanic rock formations framed the campground. As a child, Poppy thought they were the color of creamy coffee and rich, dark hot chocolate. Today marshmallow clouds floated over their tops and a hint of rain scented the air. It had been one of the coldest, wettest winters Poppy could remember. The tortoises and other desert herbivores would feast on wildflowers this spring, but in the meantime it was a bit chilly for her blood.

A ground squirrel watched hungrily from the perimeter of the campground as she unloaded Rover. Except for the crunch of gravel under her feet and an occasional bird call, the silence was complete.

Poppy stood back and surveyed her work. Red-and-white-checked cloths covered a picnic table set with midnight-blue enamel campware, tin utensils, and snowy cotton napkins. Insulated pitchers with orange juice, milk, and hot coffee occupied the center portion of the table. The drinks were flanked by a tall circular iron stand holding a dozen midnight-blue enamel cups. Covered pots of butter and jam completed the setup.

She glanced at her watch. Eight forty-five and still no sign of life in the motor homes. Well, she'd fulfilled her part of the bargain. If Josh and crew wanted to sleep the day away, it was no business of hers. She had a few minutes to explore the area around the campground.

Which way to go? The path to the right led to Hole in the Wall. To the left was an overlook into Banshee Canyon. Tall native grasses waving in the breeze seemed to beckon her in that direction.

As the sun broke through billowing clouds, she found a profusion of dandelions and even a few of her namesake desert poppies clinging to the rocky overlook. A raptor circled above the canyon. Poppy again felt a sense of oneness with this wild place. She'd never belonged anywhere until she came to live with Aunt El and Uncle Mike in Providence. Their love and the majesty of the East Mojave had filled an empty space in her heart.

"Hellooo!" A male voice floated up from the parking lot.

So, Mr. O'Donnell's internal alarm hadn't let him sleep through breakfast. She hurried back toward the campground. The sight that met her wasn't at all what she'd expected.

A sun-bronzed Josh O'Donnell stood before her. Naked to the waist, he sported a fully loaded backpack, hiking shorts, and heavy-duty boots. His upper body glistened in the morning sun.

As Poppy glanced at the empty motor homes and then back at Josh, she felt her face burn. Even more maddening was the fact that he caught her glance and correctly interpreted its meaning. She was sure she saw a smile tug the corners of Josh's lips.

"So, what's for breakfast?" he asked. "I'm starving."

Poppy busied herself rearranging the dried flowers she'd placed in an antique coffeepot in the center of the table. She needed a minute to regain her composure. What was it about the man that always threw her off balance? For one thing, it would help if he put his shirt on. The sight of his lean, smoothly muscled torso made her more than a little uneasy.

As if he had again read her thoughts, Josh dropped his backpack and pulled an olive green T-shirt from the top flap. Poppy waited until he was fully clothed before answering.

"Don't you want to wait for the others?"

"No need to wait," Josh said. He raised his voice slightly. "Poppy Sullivan, I'd like you to meet Meg Hamilton and Carlos Ruiz, my intrepid crew."

She turned to see a pair of Australian bush hats bobbing up the path. Meg looked up and grinned. Carlos waved. Both wore backpacks only slightly smaller than Josh's.

"*Exhausted* crew is more like it." Meg made a great show of huffing and puffing as she put down her pack. "Glad to meet you," she said, extending her hand.

Poppy smiled and shook it. Meg was petite like her, but of a sturdier build. She had wavy auburn hair, freckles, and one of the friendliest smiles Poppy had ever seen.

Carlos bowed slightly as he took Poppy's hand. The gesture was polite, almost courtly, but as natural as the spring breeze. She caught a glimpse of incongruously wise eyes in a smooth young face fringed with black hair.

"It's very nice to meet both of you," Poppy said. "Now, there's a dishpan full of warm soapy water on the tailgate for anyone who wants to wash up. You better hurry though. I'll have hot food on the table quicker than a fringe-toed lizard can shimmy under the sand."

Meg let out a whoop and raced for the parking lot, her exhaustion apparently forgotten. Josh wasn't far behind. Even polite Carlos joined in the chase. Soon they were all laughing and splashing each other.

Poppy couldn't help smiling at their exuberance. She liked Meg and Carlos immediately. But Josh, well, he was another story. She planned to watch Mr. Golden Eyes very closely for the next few weeks. He could be charming, no doubt about that. A little *too* charming for her taste.

Breakfast was a huge success. Poppy put heaping platters of scrambled eggs, bacon, grits, and freshly baked biscuits on the table. At the crew's urging, she joined them.

Josh and Meg kept up a lively exchange while they ate. The conversation ranged from the Amazon to South Africa and the Arctic Circle to Australia. Carlos made a comment now and then, in an accent Poppy couldn't quite place. It seemed they'd filmed in every corner of the world.

As they laughed and teased each other, Poppy began to wonder if Meg and Josh were more than fellow travelers. For some reason, the thought made Aunt El's delicious food stick in her throat. She looked up to find Carlos' quiet brown eyes watching her sympathetically.

"You'll have to excuse us, Poppy," Meg said. "Josho and I haven't worked together for over a year. We had some catching up to do."

Although the crew had been up before dawn, Meg declared there was no better way to get to know a person than over a pan of soapy water. She'd insisted on helping with the cleanup while the men relaxed in their motor homes.

"Oh. I thought you were . . . part of his regular crew," Poppy stammered.

Meg looked perplexed for a moment, then burst out laughing. "Oh, is *that* what you thought? No, no, dear. Josh and I are friends and that's all we've ever been. Although there were times when I could have cheerfully wrung his neck, I've never wanted to be romantically involved with him."

"I certainly have no interest in him," Poppy said quickly. "Our relationship is strictly business." A vision of Josh in the campground made her heart speed up. The man radiated sexuality. She wouldn't be human if she hadn't noticed. But she wanted more than good looks and a great body. She wanted things like integrity. Honor. Commitment. Things she had a feeling Mr. O'Donnell would not be able to offer.

Meg looked a doubtful. "I'm glad to hear that. Josh is a great guy but he's definitely not the type to settle down.

I have some of that wanderlust myself, so I understand it. My husband, Pete, finally found the cure for me."

Meg dried her hands on her jeans and reached into her back pocket. She produced a plastic holder filled with photos of a blue-eyed cherub. "This is Peter James Hamilton, the third. He was eighteen months old last week."

"He's adorable!" Poppy exclaimed. "I can see why you'd want to be home with him."

"Yep. I miss him already. Josho had to do some fast talking to get me signed up for this job. I promised Pete no more work out of the country, at least while P. J. is little. Pete was real sweet about taking care of him for a few weeks. My mom and a neighbor are going to pitch in too."

"From your conversation, I gather that you do the audio part of the program."

"That's right. Josh and Carlos handle the camera work. I'm the sound engineer. The nice thing about my job is that I work independently. Josh tells me what he wants—birds, rattlesnakes, lizards, environmental sounds—and I go out and get it. I don't necessarily have to record while they're filming. And *that* means a four-day work week and weekends with my family."

Poppy took another look at the photos before handing them back. "I envy you. It must be wonderful to be a mother."

"It is," Meg agreed. "But hey, it'll happen to you one of these days. You're so pretty and sweet, I'm surprised you're not married already. The way Josh was looking at you, girl, you better watch out!"

Poppy laughed. Although she had a busy life in Providence, she sometimes missed the companionship of women her own age. Most of her high school friends had moved to find jobs in bigger cities. The few that remained had married and spread out over the countryside.

"I bet women flock to him," she said.

"Like the swallows to Capistrano. But I have to give Josh credit for two things. He's choosy and he's honest. I've never seen him get involved with a woman he didn't tell right up front that he'd be moving on."

Josh watched the two women from inside the motor home. Carlos snored softly in his bunk. Drat Meg Hamilton! What was she saying to Poppy? Growing up with a sister, he'd learned something about the ways of women. He sincerely hoped Meg wasn't regaling Poppy with tales of his romantic exploits. He had enough ground to make up as it was.

Not that he was interested in a relationship with Poppy, Josh quickly assured himself. Sure, she was physically attractive, extremely appealing in her own way. But even more intriguing to him was the mind of Poppy Sullivan. He had never met anyone quite like her. She seemed so strong and rooted in her life, but at the same time possessed a childlike vulnerability.

No, getting involved with Poppy was out of the

question. She was clearly a woman who wanted more than a brief affair. If they were lucky, it could turn into a friendship. Eventually, over the miles and the years, they'd drift apart. Josh had been down that road more times than he liked to remember. Another occupational hazard, he thought, along with long hours, inclement weather, inhospitable terrain, and the occasional unfriendly advances of wild animals. Josh sighed and shrugged his shoulders. He loved his work. The other things . . . well, they came with the territory.

Still, sometimes Josh wondered if he was giving up too much for his nomad's life. He'd been out of the country for his mother's remarriage and had missed the birth of each of his three nieces. Worst of all, he'd been in the rainforests of Suriname, miles from civilization, when his father had suffered a massive brain aneurysm. Josh hadn't learned of his death until well after the funeral. In addition to grief, he'd felt guilt and an overwhelming anger at missing the chance to say goodbye. That had been three years ago. Although he'd come to terms with his guilt and rage, the sadness would always remain with him.

Now, right in front of him, was the lovely mystery of Poppy Sullivan. There was danger here, Josh realized, for both of them. But then, he had never been one to run from danger.

Poppy set a folding chair on Rover's shady side and settled down with a novel. She'd been up since the wee hours but was much too excited to nap. It was barely 11 AM and the cleanup was complete. Josh and company had certainly made quick work of Aunt El's good food. There weren't enough scraps left to satisfy the campground squirrels who had waited patiently for their portion and now eyed her accusingly.

"Sorry, little guys," Poppy said. "Better luck next time."

They scurried away at the sound of approaching footsteps. Poppy turned to see Josh striding in her direction. She was in a generous mood, buoyed by the beautiful morning and her new friendship with Meg. After all, the revelations about Josh were just as she'd expected. *I can handle him*, she decided. She greeted him with a smile as he rounded Rover's front end.

Josh returned her smile more hesitantly. He seemed rather taken aback by her friendly manner. "I, um, I thought you might like to go for a hike with me."

It was on the tip of her tongue to refuse when Josh hurried on.

"What I mean is, one of the rangers told me about a spot in Wildhorse Canyon that has some unique petroglyphs. I was hoping you'd help me find it."

Poppy thought for a minute. After all, wasn't this one of her reasons for being here? Taking a hike with Josh would give her an opportunity to observe him in the wilderness. So far, everything she'd heard from the crew impressed her. Still, it was possible Mr.

O'Donnell could be talking a respect for nature but not walking it.

"I'd love to. As long as we get back by one o'clock. I have orders to serve lunch at two."

Josh grinned, his momentary humility gone. "Sounds like you have a pretty demanding employer. Okay, I promise to have you back on time, if you can keep up the pace."

Poppy gaped at him for a moment, unable to believe her ears. The *arrogance* of the man! She jumped up so quickly that the folding chair she'd been sitting in tottered and then crashed to the ground. "We'll just see who has trouble keeping up. I'll meet you at the trailhead in ten minutes."

Josh smiled to himself as he left a hurriedly scrawled note on the picnic table for Carlos and Meg. He knew he hadn't endeared himself to Poppy with his teasing. Ah, but it had been worth it to see the fire in her eyes. Now he had two hours to get on her good side. The thought of an afternoon with Poppy Sullivan filled him with a degree of anticipation he hadn't felt in a long, long time.

Poppy was waiting when he arrived at the entrance to Hole in the Wall. The look on her face matched the dark clouds rolling overhead.

"I brought you some water." Josh held out a canteen.

"I brought my own, thank you. Only fools travel in the desert without water. Or a spare tire, for that matter."

He staggered backwards, clutching his chest. "I came with a peace offering but the fair maiden has pierced my heart. Tell me, my lady, what can I do to make amends for my knavish teasing?" He held his arms out imploringly.

"Methinks you missed your calling, Sir Josh. You should have been the court jester." Poppy turned away, but not before he saw her smile.

They climbed down iron rings set in the steep rock walls. Soon the walls widened into a canyon surrounded by towering volcanic formations riddled with holes. Straight ahead, past the fortress of Banshee Canyon, lay their destination.

"Strange names you have here," Josh said. "Hole in the Wall, Banshee Canyon, Wildhorse Canyon. Do you know any of the stories behind them?"

"Sure, but didn't the rangers already tell you?"

"They may have said something, but I'd like to hear it from a true native."

Poppy shot him a sideways glance. "I'll do my best to be colorful," she said.

"In the 1880s, a couple of cowboys from the Dominguez Ranch spotted two Indians leading what they thought were stolen cattle. They chased the Indians into a box canyon. Only, guess what? The Indians disappeared into a Hole in the Wall."

"And Banshee Canyon?"

"Named for the sound the wind makes when it whistles through these holes." As if on cue, the wind began to blow more fiercely, filling the canyon with an eerie wailing. Overhead, lightning flashed and a clap of thunder punctuated her words.

"Like now?"

"Yep. Only at night, the barn owls and great horneds that nest here add to the effect."

They were nearing the end of the rock formations. Poppy stopped to pull a flannel shirt out of her day-pack. She shouted to be heard over the approaching storm. "So, what do you say, city boy? If we go any far-ther, we're darn sure gonna get wet. Want to turn back?"

Josh looked at her, silhouetted against wide-open Wildhorse Canyon, hair whipping around her face. The sweetly pungent smell of wet creosote filled his nos-trils. Turn back now? No chance.

"Lead on, fair lady."

The wind-driven downpour caught them as they reached a pile of boulders. Poppy led the way to the sheltered side of the rocks. She pulled a tarp from her pack and motioned Josh to join her.

"You really come prepared," Josh said as they hud-dled together in the makeshift tent. "Now, tell me about Wildhorse Canyon."

Poppy glanced in Josh's direction. Damp sable hair curled enticingly around his face and the T-shirt hugged his masculine frame. She had unconsciously gravitated toward his body heat and sat thigh to thigh with him in the confined space. It was deliciously cozy there, with her smaller body pressed against his large one. Unfortunately, his closeness was making her feel a little short of breath.

"Wildhorse Canyon," Poppy began. She blew into her cupped hands and reluctantly shifted away from Josh's warmth. "That one's easy. A herd of wild horses ran through here until the sixties, when one of the local ranchers rounded them up. They say the stallion escaped, though. Black as midnight, he was, with fiery red eyes. On stormy nights you can still hear his hoof-beats thundering up the canyon." Poppy paused. "Aye, he'll spend eternity looking for his lost mares."

It was Josh's turn to applaud. "Sounds like you've spent a few evenings by the campfire yourself."

"I loved to camp in Banshee Canyon with Uncle Mike and Aunt El when I was a little girl. We'd build a roaring fire and tell ghost stories. Afterwards I slept between them in the tent. I knew nothing could harm me with them close by."

"Nobody loves a ghost story like the Irish. It must be in our blood," he said. And then quickly, "I'm sorry. I forgot that you were adopted."

"Don't be." Poppy reached over and gently placed her hand on Josh's. "I had better parents in Ella and Mike Sullivan than most children are born with. And, as luck would have it, I have some Irish blood of me own." She gave him an impish smile.

"God, you're sweet." Josh caught Poppy's hand and brought it to his lips. Soft breath feathered her skin where his lips touched her. A rush of warmth spread throughout her body. She raised her eyes to his and immediately knew it was a mistake. They were like twin pools of molten amber. So deep. So inviting.

Poppy drew a shaky breath and pulled her eyes and hand away. She wrapped her arms protectively around her knees. "It's just that I miss Uncle Mike so much."

"And I miss my father."

"Tell me about your family," she said.

Poppy's body angled toward him. Her wide blue eyes shone with sympathy. The steady rhythm of rain on their sheltering tarp added to the feeling of intimacy. Josh wondered how she'd react if he wound his fingers through her hair and pulled her to him. If he kissed her as he had longed to since the night they met. Her lips were inches away, but she looked at him with such trust, he couldn't do it. The woman had him tied in knots.

Josh wrenched his thoughts away from Poppy's lips and focused on her request.

"There's not much to tell, really. I grew up in the San Fernando Valley. My mom and dad divorced when I was thirteen. It was tough at first. I loved them both." Josh shrugged. "When you're a kid you don't have much control. You learn to accept things."

"Thirteen is such a vulnerable age. It must have been difficult for you. Do you know why they split up?" Poppy asked.

"I guess you could say they grew apart. My father was a hearty Irishman who loved the outdoors. He owned his own construction company. Mom stayed home with my sister and me until we were both in school. Then she started a career in real estate. She met new friends, had new interests. Dad developed a taste for self-pity and Irish whiskey. When I think back, I'm amazed they stayed together as long as they did."

"It's so sad when families break up," Poppy said.

"At least Mom and Dad were able to get over their hurt and anger. In fact, in their own way, I think they loved each other until the end. My dad died three years ago."

"Where are your mom and sister now?" Poppy asked.

"Mom is remarried and living in Pasadena. Elaine's still in Van Nuys. And I'm the proud uncle of three adorable little girls." Josh paused. "I'd like to hear more about your growing up years, too. Where did you live before Providence?"

A curtain descended over Poppy's open, sympathetic features. "No place special." Her guarded tone was tinged with a child's sorrow.

Josh sensed he had gotten close to the source of Poppy's vulnerability. He was about to question her further when she jumped to her feet.

"Hey, it looks like the rain's letting up." A small lake of water that had collected in the middle of the tarp poured down Josh's head and face. Poppy couldn't suppress a giggle.

"Is that any way to treat a man who's just bared his soul to you?" he sputtered.

"I'm sorry, Josh. Truly. You looked so funny." She offered her hand, which Josh pretended to regard suspiciously.

"I'll show you some pretty pictures," she coaxed.

Josh grinned. "I like the sound of that." He grabbed her hand and vaulted to his feet. "So how much farther to these petroglyphs?"

"We're here." Poppy gestured to the boulders behind them.

The downpour had obscured stylized figures carved into the boulders by an unknown Native American artist. Although the etchings were worn by wind and time, Josh could still make out people, mammals, and reptiles. His gaze lifted to a strange-looking hole in the rocks above. "What's that?" he asked, pointing.

"You're very observant. Most people don't see it." Poppy paused for a moment, as if trying to make up her mind. "Come on," she said. "I want to show you something."

A light drizzle further dampened Poppy's flannel shirt as she scrambled up the boulders. Josh couldn't help but notice the way it clung to her lithe body. At the top she raised her hands skyward, then smoothed her riotous hair. Crystalline drops fell on her upturned face.

"This is a sacred place," she murmured. "Can you feel it? The Indians came here to worship Mother Earth. They believed this place has power to heal a troubled spirit. To experience it you must pass through this life and into a new one."

Josh drank in the rain-sweet air. He let the beauty of desert, sky, and mountain wash over him. He wasn't sure if the place or Poppy's presence created the feeling of enchantment. But there was definitely something here.

She smiled and took his hand. Together they climbed the short distance to the aperture. Poppy wriggled through and motioned for Josh to follow. Although it was a tight fit, he felt no scraping or roughness. The stone, worn by the passage of countless bodies, was smooth as polished obsidian.

On the other side, Poppy waited while he regained his feet. They stood facing each other on top of the pile of boulders in the vastness of Wildhorse Canyon. Josh wasn't sure what had happened, but he felt somehow different. Refreshed, invigorated, and filled with a sense of wonder.

Poppy reached up and lightly trailed her fingers down his cheek. "Congratulations" she said softly. "You've just been reborn."

Chapter Four

He dreamed of Poppy that night. She stood on top of the boulders, arms lifted to the setting sun. Her hair streamed out in all directions, wild and untamable. Her feet, planted wide, seemed rooted in the ground. She smelled of all the sweet things of the earth. He wanted her so badly, but when she turned to him he was afraid. In his moment of hesitation, the gravel shifted beneath his feet. He began to slide down the hill. Poppy held her arms out imploringly, her expression begging him to stay. But he couldn't. Farther and farther he slid, until he could no longer see her. Then came the sensation of falling, falling into darkness.

It had been a wild night. He had said goodbye to Poppy in a light drizzle. By midnight the wind howled through the canyon and rain pounded their flimsy

53

metal shelters. Josh got up once to check on Meg, then spent the rest of the night tossing and turning. It seemed he'd just fallen asleep when Carlos gently shook him.

"Boss. It's time to get up."

Groaning, Josh rolled out of his bunk. He grabbed a towel and stumbled down the motor home stairs, feeling as sore and bleary-eyed as if he'd been on a three-day drunk. Yes, he'd been drunk, he decided as he groped through the predawn darkness toward the campground's only water faucet. But not on alcohol.

Josh sputtered and blew as cold water streamed over his head and face. He turned off the faucet, then raised his head in time to see Meg and Carlos exchange an amused look, illuminated by their Coleman lantern. There was no hiding anything from those two. They knew him too well to have missed the fact that he was thoroughly infatuated with Poppy Sullivan.

Bewitched was more like it, Josh thought grumpily. Against his will and much against his better judgment.

The morning passed quickly. Josh and Carlos filmed a coyote hunting in the early light. Later they observed a two-foot-long Gila monster sunning himself in a spectacular devil's garden. The fat black-and-red lizard blinked at them lazily, seeming more annoyed than frightened by their presence.

Although the devil's garden combination of rocks and cacti was typical for this community of drought-resistant creosote bushes and low desert shrubs, the

Gila monster was a rare find. Josh was elated when they returned to camp.

"Hello," Poppy called. "Did you sleep well?"

Josh suspected for a moment that she was teasing, but Poppy's face was devoid of guile. In fact, in a red gingham shirt and snug jeans, she looked about sixteen years old. The wild hair he remembered was pulled back in a tight braid, secured by a red band. Josh wondered if the incredible experience they'd shared in Wildhorse Canyon was a figment of his storm-tossed dreams.

As he drew nearer, Josh saw distress behind Poppy's smile. Carlos, ever sensitive and considerate, made an excuse and retreated to the motor home.

"Can I talk to you for a minute?" Poppy twisted a button on her shirt nervously.

"Sure." Josh plopped down at the picnic table. He set his hat carefully on the bench so as not to disturb the pretty place settings.

"It's about yesterday. I hope you're not planning to include the ceremonial ground in your documentary. I haven't shown it to many people. Actually, I haven't shown it to anyone but you. I don't know what came over me. I'm not usually so impulsive." Poppy remained standing during this speech and nearly twisted the button off her shirt.

Josh patted the rough wood beside him. "Sit next to me."

She perched on the far end of the picnic bench, looking as relaxed as a hen in a barnyard full of roosters. When had he become so intimidating? Josh wondered.

He straddled the bench and took Poppy's hands in his. "First of all, I wouldn't even consider including the place you showed me in the documentary. I know there are people in this world who have no respect for cultural artifacts or native religions. There aren't many unspoiled sites like that left, and it's our responsibility to protect them. Second, I am touched and honored that you chose to share your special place with me. It was an afternoon I'll never forget."

Poppy looked up through her lashes and gave him a sassy smile. "You know, for a city boy, you're not so bad."

Josh grinned back. "I consider that a great compliment."

Each day Poppy spent with Josh and his crew was an education. She learned they were on location thirty minutes before dawn every morning. During midday, Josh frequently made calls on his cell phone, did a rough edit of the morning's footage, or wrote in his journal. About 4 P.M., when Poppy drove home, they headed back into the canyon to take advantage of the late afternoon light.

Despite their demanding schedule, Josh, Meg, and Carlos always found time to share their expertise with Poppy. Josh told her about post-production procedures. Meg played back some recordings and explained how they were mixed in the studio. Carlos gave her a hands-on lesson in the workings of his Arriflex camera. In return, Poppy shared her unique knowledge of the East Mojave Desert. When they said goodbye for the weekend, Poppy felt like one of the gang.

Monday dawned clear and brilliant. Although Rover's radio had long ago given out, Poppy provided her own musical accompaniment by tapping the steering wheel and humming snatches of popular tunes. She was headed for one of her favorite places, the Kelso Dunes, where Outback Productions would film that week.

These sand dunes were among the few worldwide noted for their booming effect. When conditions were right, vibrations could be both heard and felt while sliding down the face of the dunes. Poppy hoped the sand had dried enough after last week's storm to hum along with her.

A gay yellow-and-white striped beach cabana cast a rectangle of shade on the sand just north of the Kelso Dunes parking area. Good, he hadn't forgotten. Josh promised to provide the shelter for their meals, but just in case, Poppy had brought a couple of the oversized beach umbrellas she and Aunt El used during their summer vacations.

A slight breeze ruffled the cabana, bringing with it bittersweet memories of the vacations her family had spent at Aunt Maureen's in San Diego. Uncle Mike and

Aunt El always closed the store during the hottest month of the summer to enjoy some cool coastal breezes. For the last two years she and Aunt El had gone alone.

Shaking off the moment of sadness, Poppy unloaded a couple of card tables from Rover's sagging back end. Aunt El had outdone herself today. She'd packed two different quiches and fresh scones, along with a jar of the prickly pear jelly she'd put up last spring. Lunch wasn't any lighter: fried chicken, potato salad, green salad, ranch-style pinto beans, cornbread, and for dessert, sweet potato pie. Poppy knew that somehow the hungry crew would polish it off.

The beach cabana and red and blue umbrellas looked like a cluster of giant blossoms in the sand. Poppy put two card tables under the cabana and spread them with red-and-white-checked cloths.

In the distance, three small figures approached. She climbed onto a chair to wave and the lead figure waved back. Josh must have been watching for her, Poppy realized with a glow of pleasure. Her opinion of him had certainly changed in a week's time. He was handsome and self-assured, no doubt about that. But the arrogance she had first assumed was missing. If anything, Josh was quite modest about his accomplishments. He was simply a man who loved his work and did it very, very well. She had also become convinced that Josh had a genuine love for wild places and the creatures who inhabited them.

Although he had been friendly but proper during the preceding week, several times she'd felt his intense gaze on her. Once, when she looked up, he'd given her a lazy grin that turned her insides to butter. The very air around the man seemed to pulse with sensuality.

Despite his effect on her—and undoubtedly many other women—Poppy no longer believed that Josh's charm was calculated. He was just being Josh. Poppy found herself beginning to like and admire him. *Much more than I should*, she thought, hopping down from the chair. His love-'em-and-leave-'em reputation was undoubtedly well deserved.

Poppy shook off her forebodings. It was a glorious spring day and she had never felt more alive. She grinned and waved again as the threesome drew closer.

Josh couldn't believe what a pretty picture Poppy made smiling from under the cabana. She looked like a high school cheerleader in cutoff jeans and a blue T shirt that brought out the sapphire in her eyes. Everything about her was neat and pressed. Wholesome. Everything except the multitude of brown curls that had escaped from a high ponytail and now danced around her face. He wondered for a moment how it would feel to see that fresh face waiting for him at the end of each day. But that dream belonged to another man's life, not his.

"Good morning, sunshine," he said.

"Ah, Mr. O'Donnell, and how are you this fine morning?"

"Hungry enough to eat everything on that table," he replied, "and then gobble you up for dessert."

Poppy's eyes sparkled with mischief. "Oh, pray, sir, don't do that. There's more food in the truck if this isn't enough for you. And besides, I'm much too skinny to bother with."

That was a matter of opinion, Josh thought. "All right, I'll spare you this time. But only because Carlos and Meg would stake me to an anthill if anything happened to you or Aunt El's chow. That stuff is addicting. What are we having, anyway?" Josh lifted a corner of the dish towel covering a basket of freshly baked scones.

Poppy slapped his hand. "Not until you've washed up and Meg and Carlos get here," she said firmly. "I still have to set out the hot dishes."

"Ow!" Josh rubbed his wounded hand. "If I faint from hunger you'll be sorry."

"I'll take my chances."

Breakfast was filled with news of the weekend and plans for the days ahead. Poppy asked if they had heard any booming on the dunes during their morning shoot.

"Not yet," Josh answered. "I'm told a warm, dry day provides the optimum conditions." He hesitated. "I thought I might go back out this afternoon, if you'd like to join me. Of course, you're both welcome to come, too," Josh added, glancing at Meg and Carlos.

Meg yawned and stretched. "No way," she said. "I've got a date with my bunk this afternoon. P. J. was up and down all night, teething." Meg sighed and rolled her eyes. "But hey, you two go ahead. Carlos and I will clean up."

"Oh, no, I couldn't let you . . ." Poppy started to protest.

"Listen, I need to get up and move around a little bit, let my food digest. I'm as full as a tick. We're happy to do it, aren't we, Carlos?"

"Very happy, Senorita Poppy." Carlos nodded and smiled. He and Meg exchanged a conspiratorial look whose meaning was all too easy to interpret.

"It looks like you're outvoted," Josh said.

"Well, I'll just go get my pack. Thanks." Poppy smiled uncertainly and scurried away, hoping to hide her blush. It was one thing to joke around with Josh at the campsite with Meg and Carlos close by, quite another to be alone with him in the wilderness again.

Poppy's face grew warmer as she remembered her behavior during their last outing. That really wasn't like her. The intimacy of their shelter and Josh's willingness to share painful childhood memories had made her forget her reservations. She had the feeling it was something he didn't do often, just as she was reluctant to share her own early memories, even with her closest friends.

She returned to the picnic area in a pensive mood. Meg and Carlos had already cleared the table. She could hear the sound of their low voices, punctuated by running water and the clink of dishes coming from Meg's motor home.

"Thanks, guys," she called.

Meg's head popped out the door. "You'd better get going. It looks like a primo day for rumbling sands."

The sun was climbing higher in a sky as blue as a robin's egg. Poppy judged the temperature to be in the low eighties. She was glad she'd put on plenty of sunscreen. Although she loved the ancient, leathery desert tortoises, she didn't want to end up resembling one.

She and Josh walked for a while in silence. As they traversed a small dune and lost sight of the camp, Josh stopped abruptly. "I have something for you," he said. He pulled off his backpack and extracted an Australian bush hat just like his, only brand new.

"Why, Josh, thank you!" Poppy gave him a quick kiss on the cheek. Although the sun was warm, it didn't account for the fiery feeling in her lips as they touched his skin. He smelled of sage and sunshine with a hint of bay rum. Poppy took a faltering step backwards. She felt as if an electrical current had passed between them.

One look at Josh told her he felt it, too. His gaze seared her. It was the same hungry look she remembered seeing the night they met. It frightened her, but at the same time ignited a desire that leaped up to match his own. Poppy held the hat in front of her like a shield as she attempted to regain her composure.

"It was so sweet of you to think of me. Wherever did you find this?" she asked.

Josh shrugged. "There's a little Australian import

store in the L.A. area. You've become like one of the crew, so I thought you should have it."

Poppy put the hat on with trembling hands. "How do I look?" she asked.

"Like water in a parched land."

The compliment filled her with a delicious but uneasy warmth. *What a silver-tongued devil,* she thought. His pretty words, along with the handsome face and muscular body, were enough to turn any woman's head.

Poppy fell back a step or two as they climbed the dunes. She had no trouble keeping up, but needed a little time to regain her equilibrium. No doubt about it, Josh O'Donnell was a dangerous man. If she could bottle his sex appeal, she'd be able to buy a fleet of four-wheel-drive vehicles. But could she bear to part with any of it?

She smiled at the thought. If only she were able to enjoy the excitement of falling for Josh without the inevitable consequences. As surely as she lived and breathed, there could only be one end to loving him: a broken heart.

They stopped several times to catch their breath or point out tiny footprints in the sand. Lizards, roadrunners, and kangaroo rats were frequent travelers here. Once they came upon the distinctive J-shaped imprints of a sidewinder rattlesnake.

At this time of day, everything that moved and breathed had taken cover from the sun. Everything except the two of them. Josh and Poppy plunged knee-deep in sand with each step, losing ground as the ascent grew steeper. After much slipping and sliding, they reached the top. The view made it all worthwhile.

To the north, the Kelso Mountains. The Bristol Mountains to the southwest, the Granite Mountains to the south, and to the east, Poppy's beloved Providence Range. They plopped down and took long drinks from their water bottles while replenishing their spirits with the grandeur of the expansive East Mojave.

"Poppy," Josh said.

"Yes?" She turned from nature's wonder to regard her companion. He'd rolled her name over his tongue like an unfamiliar but tasty dessert.

"I was just wondering how you got your name. I've never heard it before."

"Actually, it's Penelope," Poppy screwed up her face as she pronounced the word. "When I first met Uncle Mike and Aunt El, I was a skinny little thing. All eyes and hair, Uncle Mike said. Anyway, he said Penelope was too long a handle for such a little girl. He named me for the wild desert poppies that bloom in the spring. When Uncle Mike and Aunt El brought me to Providence, the first thing I saw was a big banner across the front of the store. It said 'Poppy's Place.' And it's been home ever since."

Josh smiled. "That's a nice story. Like the poppies, you blossomed in the desert."

"Funny, that's just what Uncle Mike said. Although,

if Aunt El had her way I'd have blossomed a whole lot
more. She's been trying to 'put some meat on my
bones' since I was in pigtails and hula hoops. I'm afraid
I've been a big disappointment."

Josh laughed. "Well, if it helps any, I think your
bones are perfect just the way they are."

Poppy's eyes shone with pleasure. Her hat was tilted
back, framing her lovely, open face. Josh touched her
cheek and saw her eyes widen slightly, but she didn't
pull away. He couldn't help himself. He leaned forward
and claimed her lips with his own.

"Poppy," he murmured, pulling the hat from her
head. She shivered despite the warmth of the day and
leaned into him. Stroking her face, he kissed her gently, two, three times. Her eyes were closed, her mouth
warm and yielding. He took her in his arms and pressed
her body to his. She was sweet, so sweet. Just as he had
imagined that first night in the desert.

Poppy's arms came around his neck and she whim-
pered softly as their kiss deepened. Her mouth, at first
compliant, became bolder and more inquisitive.

Josh knew he couldn't stand much more.

"Hold on, sunshine," he said. "We're going for a
ride."

Poppy barely heard him. She was lost in the feel, the
smell, the taste of Josh. Suddenly she felt her weight
shift. Josh had rolled on top of her. Then she was on top
of him. They were rolling down the dune!

Poppy let out a small squeal and lifted her gaze from

the curve of Josh's neck. First she saw the flash of the sun, then the gleam in his eyes. His mouth was curled in a devilish grin. Over and over they rolled. His arms held her so tightly that their bodies seemed as one. She had never experienced such a dizzying sensation.

Beneath them, Poppy felt and heard the vibration of the sand. It wasn't exactly a hum. More like the sound of bumblebees. Or kettle drums. On this day, it was a crescendo for a symphony of sensation. The motion of their bodies gradually slowed as the dune leveled. Finally they stopped. Neither one moved. They looked at each other wide-eyed, then burst into laughter.

Josh's shirt was twisted to one side and his eyes sparkled. After their slide down the dune he still managed to look rakishly charming. She could only imagine how she looked.

He stood and offered his hand. "Sweetheart, that was one heck of a ride."

Poppy nodded shakily. Her heart pounded like she'd run a five-minute mile. She accepted his hand up and began brushing at her clothes, more for something to do than because she had any hope of restoring order. She pulled her hair into a quick ponytail and secured it at the nape of her neck.

"What about our hats and backpacks?" she asked.

"Don't worry. Carlos and I will pick them up this evening. Right now, we'd better get back to camp. I think we've had enough excitement for one day."

Poppy suddenly felt shy. Her hand was firmly

encased in Josh's as they walked down the gentle slope. She'd done it again, only this time she'd completely lost control. If they hadn't tumbled down the dune, who knows what would have happened? Then she figured it out. That tumble had been no accident. She stopped and stared accusingly at Josh.

"You did that on purpose!"

"Poppy, Poppy." He said her name caressingly but with just a hint of teasing. "A man can only take so much . . . uh, stimulation. Even on top of a sand dune in the middle of the day. I thought I'd better get things on a different track and at the moment, that seemed the best way to go. You have to admit, it was fun."

Fun was not the word she would have chosen for their wild ride. Sensuous, startling, spine-tingling, maybe. It had shaken her to the core, awakened all her senses. She still felt slightly dizzy, and not just from rolling down the dune. She'd never met a man who made her feel quite so alive. It was a wonderful feeling, but at the same time, a little frightening. "It was incredible."

They continued walking for a while in silence. "I didn't mean to tease you," she said.

"Nor I you. I'm tremendously attracted to you, Poppy. I think you know that. But our lives are so different. I don't stay in one place very long."

"So I've heard."

"Meg?"

Poppy nodded. "She also told me you'd never gotten

involved with a woman you didn't tell right up front that you'd be moving on."

"I don't want to hurt you, Poppy."

"I'm a big girl, Josh. I can take care of myself."

The words were out now, in the open. But did she really mean them? Poppy wondered. She had a lot to think about on the drive back to Providence.

The gravel lot in front of Poppy's Place was empty. As Poppy drew closer, she saw the CLOSED sign hanging in the window. Although the cafe stopped serving meals at two o'clock, the store and gas pumps should have been open. Could Aunt El be sick?

She bounded up the front steps and threw open the door, letting the screen slam behind her.

"I swear, child. You look as though the devil himself is after you." Aunt El sat at one of the cafe tables, leafing through a magazine. A neatly wrapped foil package rested on the table in front of her. She picked up her coat and began to put it on.

Poppy stared at her, open-mouthed. Aunt El never went anywhere in the evening. In fact, except for a weekly shopping expedition, she was content to let the world come to her.

"Uh, are you going somewhere?"

El looked at Poppy like she was a lovable but slow-witted child. "Aye."

Poppy persisted. "What's in the package?"

"A pie."

"A pie? Ohhhh, a *pie!*" Suddenly it all became clear. Aunt El was delivering a pie. To Homer Bell. "Would you like me to drive you?"

"No, darlin'. You stay here. Treat yourself to a bubble bath. I think the folks in Providence can do without us for one evening."

"I'm sure Homer will be glad to see you," Poppy said. "Do you know how to get to his house?"

El nodded. "Mary Evans stopped by the store today. You know, the oldest of Dusty Evans' girls? She said some of their bunch have been working for Mr. Bell, building a deck around his mobile home. She gave me directions to his place."

Poppy tried not to look worried. "Drive carefully."

"Don't worry, darlin'. I'll just make my apology and come home. The poor man hasn't been in the cafe for a week now. I can't bear to think I've hurt him." Aunt El belted her coat tightly, squared her shoulders, and sailed through the door.

Chapter Five

"Poppy, dear, I'm making scones this morning and I'd like to send some home to Josh's mother. Ask him to stop by after work, will you?" Aunt El adjusted her glasses, smudging one rosy cheek with flour.

Poppy narrowed her eyes at her adopted mom. "You're sending scones to Josh's mother?"

"And what's wrong with that, I'd like to know?"

"Nothing, I guess." Nothing except that she could feel in her bones that Aunt El was up to something. The innocent act didn't fool her for a minute. "Are you sure you don't have an ulterior motive for inviting Josh over here?"

"Humph!" Aunt El snorted. "Since when do I need an *ulterior motive* to give away scones? As it happens, I've become very fond of that young man and he told

70

me his mother is partial to scones. Now, are you going to deliver the message? Or do I have to stand on the highway and flag him down?"

The mental image of Aunt El standing beside old Route 66, apron flapping in the breeze, was too much for Poppy. She rolled her eyes and grinned. "You win. I'll tell him." She blew Aunt El a kiss as she hurried out the door.

Just as Poppy suspected, Aunt El had more on her mind than pastry. Josh arrived at the cafe shortly after noon on Friday to receive a box of freshly baked scones and an invitation to Sunday dinner, which he accepted.

Poppy wasn't sure whether to be aggravated or pleased. She didn't have much time to dwell on the matter. The peak season for visitors to the national preserve was beginning. Even with extra help she and Aunt El were busy all weekend.

On Sunday afternoon, with the restaurant closed and Aunt El preparing dinner, Poppy stood ankle-deep in a pile of rejected clothing. The sleeveless cotton dress she'd bought in San Diego last summer was a little too dressy for dinner at home. She didn't want to appear overly eager. Her khaki shorts, maybe? No, too grunge. How about jeans and a silk blouse?

Poppy caught a glimpse of her worried expression in the mirror. She plopped down on her bed and shook her head. What was happening to her? She hadn't felt this way since high school, getting ready for a dance. She had the same tingling sensation in the pit of her stomach, the same irrational but unshakeable feeling that tonight she would meet her hero.

How often she had imagined him. He'd be dependable, gentle, honest and straightforward. He'd share her love for the East Mojave and want to raise a family here. He'd be a man who placed her needs above his own, a man who knew the meaning of honor, integrity and commitment.

A man who . . . was not Josh O'Donnell.

"You've been watching too many old movies," Poppy muttered. She grabbed a pair of worn, form-fitting jeans and a white rib-knit shell from the pile on the floor. A brightly woven Guatemalan belt added a dash of color. At the last minute, she slipped on a sterling silver charm bracelet. It was her magic talisman, worn on all the special occasions in her life.

Not that I expect tonight to be special, she told herself. Sure, Josh was attractive, and he wasn't as unscrupulous as she had first believed. But he was entirely too footloose and fancy-free. Not at all the type she was looking for. If she could only remember that when he got within ten feet of her.

She wandered into their sunny private dining room to take a last look at the table she'd prepared earlier. The cafe's blue and white dishes looked elegant against a white linen cloth set with Aunt El's good silver. Large windows framed the flower and herb beds

Poppy maintained year-round. A vase of freshly cut pansies in red, pink, and purple provided the crowning touch.

With over an hour left before Josh's arrival, Poppy followed her nose into the kitchen.

Aunt El stood at the long kitchen counter spread with numerous herbs and spices, milk, and eggs. It had always amazed Poppy how she could blend so many different ingredients into several dishes and have everything ready at the same time.

"Mmmm! What's that heavenly smell?"

Aunt El turned. "My, don't you look lovely," she said. "Chicken cutlets with raspberries, white and wild rice, and spring vegetables in a lemon butter sauce. For dessert we're having creme de caramel."

"I don't know how you do it," Poppy said, shaking her head in admiration. "You could have been a chef in a five-star restaurant."

"Ah, but then my recipes would have lacked the most important ingredients: love and affection."

Poppy put her arm around Aunt El's shoulders and gave a quick squeeze. "I'm glad you invited him," she whispered.

Aunt El stopped chopping to return the hug. "I know, darlin'."

"By the way, how was your date with Homer last night?" Poppy grinned, hoping to get a rise out of her. She wasn't disappointed.

"For your information, Miss Smartypants, it wasn't a

date. Homer—that is, Mr. Bell—is writing a volume of poetry about the desert. I'm helping with his research."

"Oh, poetry, is it? They wouldn't be love poems, would they?" Poppy was surprised to see the pink in Aunt El's cheeks spread to her hairline. Immediately contrite, she changed the subject. "Did you find out why he only stays an hour in the cafe?"

Aunt El looked at Poppy for a minute as if trying to decide on an answer. She stood up straighter and her voice took on a note of pride. "He says he comes for inspiration. Now skedaddle so I can get supper on the table."

Well, if that doesn't take the cake. Aunt El was keeping company with Homer Bell. From what she'd seen of Homer, he was a gentle, quiet soul, much different than her garrulous Uncle Mike. Still, Aunt El had a glow about her that Poppy hadn't seen since Mike died.

She grabbed a handful of crackers and a bag of washed broccoli from the refrigerator, then skipped out the door.

"Holler if you need any help," she called, knowing full well Aunt El wouldn't. Although El had tried her best, Poppy had never had the patience to learn her culinary secrets. From the day she'd arrived in Providence, Poppy had spent every spare moment in the great outdoors.

The grapevines separating their backyard from the gravel parking lot were beginning to leaf out. Poppy turned the sprinkler on low. Conditions were just about perfect for her tortoises to emerge from their long hibernation. She hoped the smell of water would coax them from their burrows. *Any day now*, she thought. She'd added the tortoises' favorite food, broccoli, to sweeten the deal.

Poppy sat on the bench at the far end of the yard, soaking up the late afternoon sun. Just a few weeks ago, in this very spot, she'd said yes to Josh's business proposition. It seemed like so much longer. But as Poppy knew, a few weeks in springtime could bring many changes.

She began to crumble crackers and toss them to a pair of robins who had built their nest in a mulberry tree. Mama and papa must have a lot of hungry mouths to feed, she thought. She loved to watch the pair hop about, looking for worms and tasty insects. They were always so busy in the spring.

Poppy wondered, as she had so often in the past, if she'd ever have a baby of her own. She had always loved children and animals. She felt a special empathy for small, defenseless creatures. While she was growing up, hardly a week had gone by when she wasn't caring for some sick, injured, or orphaned critter in this back-yard. But to have a child, a small human being who called her Mom—that would really be something.

"A penny for your thoughts."

Poppy turned quickly to see Josh lounging in the doorway. She jumped up and brushed the crumbs from her jeans, suddenly feeling fluttery and disoriented, like a fledgling blown from its nest. Darn that man! How long had he been watching her? Determined not to let Josh see his effect on her, Poppy took a deep breath and gave him her most dazzling smile.

"Step into my parlor and I'll share my innermost secrets and desires . . . but only if you go first."

Josh laughed and ambled over to where she was sitting. "Just like a woman to test the waters before diving in."

"How do you know so much about women?" Poppy challenged.

"Direct observation. You forget, my dear, I have an older sister. And there was never a peskier little brother than me."

"That I believe. You seem to have a talent for sneaking up on people."

"People and animals," he agreed. "The many hours I spent spying on Elaine have proved invaluable to my career as a wildlife cinematographer. Now, about those innermost secrets . . ."

"Look!" Poppy exclaimed in a hushed voice. "It's Lillian." She touched Josh's arm and nodded in the direction of one of the long earthen berms. The head and front quarters of a desert tortoise protruded from its opening.

"Well, I'll be darned," Josh said. "Is this her debut?"

"Yep, first time this spring. Good thing I came prepared." Poppy walked slowly over to the tortoise.

Lillian was tearing off great mouthfuls of the wet green grass.

"Hello there, sleepyhead. Where are your friends?" She broke off a broccoli floweret and set it in front of the tortoise, softly stroking Lillian's head when she stretched it toward the treat.

"She seems pretty tame," Josh said.

"Lillian was a pet tortoise, collected from the desert. The people kept her in a box in their house and fed her lettuce. It's one of the worst foods you can give a tortoise. They love it but it has very little nutritional value. At least the owners were kind enough to bring Lillian to the Friends when she became sick and malnourished. In a few more months she'll be ready for adoption, to a home where people know how to care for her."

"Look, here comes another one," Josh said.

"Clara. Welcome to the world." Poppy and Josh stood still while Clara lumbered toward them. Soon Myrna joined the others for a long drink of water and a feast of grass and broccoli. Lillian stood under the sprinkler, seeming to enjoy the gentle shower.

"Now what was it you were saying about females being afraid to dive in?" Poppy teased.

"I was speaking figuratively. Where's Valentino?"

"Sleeping in, I guess. You remembered his name."

"I remember everything you say to me."

They were standing close together. So close she caught the tang of his aftershave and felt the warmth emanating from his muscular frame. Poppy felt the tiny hairs on her arms stand up. Tentatively, she raised her eyes to Josh's. He was looking at her so strangely, she thought for a moment he was going to kiss her. Instead, he took her hand and said in a husky voice, "We should go see about dinner."

They walked hand in hand across the yard in the early spring twilight. At the door, Josh turned and said, "You never told me what you were thinking."

Poppy considered her answer. Should she tell Josh she'd been wishing for a child of her own? He'd only be in Providence for a few more weeks. No sense in scaring the daylights out of the man. She withdrew her hand and opened the back door. "I was thinking about the changes springtime brings."

Soft Irish folk music played in the background and long, tapering white candles rose gracefully from crystal holders in the center of the table. A note from Aunt El nestled against the centerpiece. It read: *I was feeling a little tired so decided to turn in early. Dinner's in the oven. Enjoy your evening.*

"I swear, she's incorrigible!" Poppy said.

"I'm not complaining." Josh gave Poppy's hand a squeeze. "I'll light the candles."

Josh watched as Poppy poured them each a glass of Chardonnay. She looked even younger by the flickering candlelight. Young and sweet and oh, so desirable. He'd spent the weekend anticipating this evening, hardly

daring to hope for a few moments alone with her. Now
Aunt El, bless her, had given him the entire evening. So
why couldn't he relax?

He knew, of course. Poppy aroused feelings he didn't
quite understand and wasn't prepared to deal with. She
was the marrying kind. He'd sensed that from the
beginning. With her softness and warmth, her nurturing
instinct, of course she'd want a family. What could be
more natural for a young woman like Poppy? Or more
foreign to his way of life.

He wanted Poppy. More than he'd ever wanted any
woman. Not just physically, although that in itself was
a powerful longing. He wanted to possess her, body,
mind, and spirit. He wanted to unlock the secrets of her
heart.

And then what? Josh asked himself. Be on my way
to Nepal or Nigeria or Singapore? Leaving Poppy
behind to pick up the pieces. No, he couldn't do that to
her. As much as he desired Poppy, the urge to protect
her was stronger still.

"Have I grown a pair of horns?" Poppy asked.

"I beg your pardon?" Josh blinked at her in surprise.

"The way you were staring at me, I thought maybe
I'd sprouted horns."

I'm the one with horns, and a forked tail to match,
Josh thought. "Sorry. It's a bad habit of mine."

"I don't mind, really. That intense look is part of
your charm." Poppy tilted her head to one side and gave
him a smile that was half shy and half teasing. Her eyes

shone with a warmth that could not be entirely attrib-
uted to candlelight.

Dear God, give me strength, Josh thought.

"Shall we drink a toast?" Poppy asked. She lightly
touched her glass to his. "To a lovely evening."

As the twilight deepened, they sipped wine and
munched warm honey wheat bread spread with sweet
butter. Out in the yard, the tortoise harem headed back
into their burrows. Soon the only illumination was provided by the candles' flames. It reminded Josh of the
first evening he'd spent with Poppy, opposite a campfire. Even then, he'd known she was someone special.

Poppy heated Aunt El's raspberry sauce and drizzled
it over the still-warm chicken cutlets. The aroma of
raspberries, lemon, and herbs preceded her into the
dining room. As she bent to serve him, Josh caught a
whiff of Poppy's perfume. It was sweet and warm, like
sunshine with a hint of vanilla. He wanted to kiss all the
secret places from which the scent emanated. With
great effort, Josh forced himself to concentrate on the
plate Poppy set in front of him.

"It looks wonderful," he said. "Did you make it?"

Poppy smiled her thanks as Josh jumped up to seat
her. "I'm afraid cooking isn't one of my talents."

"Tell me about them."

"My talents? I guess interests would be a better
word. I love the outdoors. I'm interested in the desert's
plants and animals. And I enjoy watching things grow.
I planted our flower and herb gardens." Poppy gestured

toward the tidy plots in the darkening yard. "I love children. I considered being a teacher for a while. I'd just finished my AA degree at the community college in Barstow when Uncle Mike died."

"And then?"

"Then I came home. Although she wouldn't admit it, I knew Aunt El needed me in the store."

"You gave up your dream to help your aunt?"

"Not gave up. Postponed, maybe. Someday we hope to have an elementary school in Providence. I'd like to teach."

Josh was silent as he considered what Poppy had told him. They were different in so many ways. Like her beloved tortoises, Poppy belonged here. He didn't belong anywhere. Even his apartment in Los Angeles was little more than a place to rest between trips. He'd collected boxes of souvenirs, mementos of his travels, but had never gotten around to displaying them. The walls of his bachelor apartment were as bare as when he'd moved in five years ago.

"And what about you?" Poppy asked. "Will you always be a rolling stone?"

"My work demands it," said Josh. "And truthfully, I can't imagine any other life. Traveling to a new location every few months, getting to know the local culture, the wildlife, and the climate, overcoming whatever challenges they have to offer. It's like an addiction. It gets into your blood. I haven't been in one place for more than six months since I left Van Nuys."

"And just where do love and affection fit into your life, Mr. O'Donnell?"

"I try to be grateful for what I am offered freely," Josh replied. "Despite what Meg may have told you, my romantic exploits are hardly on par with Don Juan's."

Poppy laughed and touched her glass to Josh's. "Well spoken, Sir Josh. Now eat your dinner while I ponder the consequences of consorting with a wandering knave such as yourself."

Whether it was the wine or the magical effect of Aunt El's cooking, Poppy couldn't say. Somehow her earlier nervousness was gone, replaced by a glow of contentment and well-being. She watched as Josh enjoyed the repast, candlelight shimmering in his hair. She remembered how that hair felt against her face in the heat of the noonday sun. Whatever their differences in lifestyle, whatever tomorrow might bring, she and Josh had this special evening together. She was determined that nothing would spoil it.

"Would you like to have dessert in the family room?" Poppy asked. "I thought we might watch an old movie. Unless you need to get to bed. I know you have an early morning."

Josh looked into her hopeful blue eyes and knew he should go. His conscience said, "Leave while you still can," but somehow his lips formed the words, "I'd love to."

He offered to help clean up but Poppy wouldn't hear

of it. Josh was left with nothing to do but sip the last of his wine and wonder what had happened to him. He'd lost control of his own actions. Had Aunt El put something in the raspberry sauce? Or was it Poppy who had bewitched him? He suspected the latter was true. Watching her now as she darted between the table and kitchen, he remembered his dream not so many nights ago. She had seemed to embody love, comfort, sustenance, passion, everything he desired. He'd felt so lost when he couldn't reach her.

Josh shook his head hard. Thank goodness Poppy was busy in the kitchen. If she'd seen him, she'd have thought he was a lunatic. Unrequited physical attraction had him behaving like a lovesick rhinoceros.

Maybe it was time to stop fighting it, he thought. Despite her girlish appearance, Poppy was a grown woman. He'd been very clear about the limitations of their relationship. She was capable of making her own decision.

Josh got up and pushed his chair under the table. He crossed to where Poppy stood at the sink, up to her elbows in frothy, iridescent bubbles. Her back was to him and running water covered the sound of his approach. The air was fragrant with the fresh, clean scent of soap. Beneath it, he caught a hint of Poppy's warm vanilla essence.

He did what he'd been longing to do all evening. He put his arms around her and gently pressed his lips to the vulnerable spot behind her ear. He inhaled her scent and tasted the sweetness of her skin. The curls at Poppy's neck caressed his cheek with downy softness.

She started momentarily, then relaxed against him. Although her head barely reached his shoulder, her body seemed to meld perfectly to his. Josh felt his pulse quicken as the softness of her body inflamed him with a painfully sweet desire.

He'd been right. She wanted him as much as he wanted her. He'd lost the ability to think about consequences. All that mattered was holding Poppy in his arms tonight.

Josh was half reclining on the couch when Poppy came into the family room. His golden eyes followed her every move. She set the tray holding their decafs and dessert on the coffee table and offered Josh a tentative smile.

The only light filtered through gauzy curtains from the back porch. Poppy busied herself straightening stacks of videos while she tried to slow her heartbeat and calm the now-familiar flutter deep within her.

"Is there anything you'd especially like to see?" she asked. "Aunt El has quite a collection. Bette Davis, Joan Crawford, practically everything Bogart and Bacall made. I love their first movie together."

"To Have and Have Not," Josh said. "You don't have to say anything and you don't have to do anything. Just whistle."

Poppy laughed and expelled a whoosh of breath she

hadn't realized she'd been holding. "Hey, I think that was my line."

Josh removed a long leg from the seat so she could join him. His arm remained stretched across the back of the couch. The open collar of his shirt revealed a glimpse of bronzed chest, covered with a fine sheen of gold-tipped hair. Poppy had a sudden longing to run her fingers over its springy softness.

"Come here, sweetheart," he rasped in a better-than average Bogey imitation.

Poppy picked up a spoon and dessert dish, then nestled against him on the couch. "You have to try some of Aunt El's creme de caramel," she said. "It's heaven in a cup."

She was right. The chilled spoon Poppy slipped into his mouth held a potion so deeply rich and creamy, Josh thought his taste buds might never recover. He closed his eyes to savor the sensation of delectably light custard and sweet, tangy caramel gliding over his palate. Slowly, he traced his lips with his tongue. "Now you," he said.

Poppy closed her eyes and inclined her face toward him, her lips slightly parted. But instead of cold metal, they encountered a warm mouth, tasting of strong, sensual male and sweet caramel. Oh, how that man loved to tease!

She cupped his face, exploring the strong bones of his cheek and jaw. His mouth covered hers with sweet, seductive kisses. Kisses that made her senses tingle and her body ache for more.

"You're a dangerous man, Josh O'Donnell," she whispered.

His smile flashed in the semi-darkness. "And you, Penelope Sullivan, are the most desirable woman I've ever met." He shifted so Poppy was leaning back against his chest. As he wrapped his arms around her, his fingertips brushed the charm bracelet at her wrist.

"What have we here?" Josh lifted her hand close to his face so he could see the charms. "A snake, a fox, a pair of cowboy boots, a tortoise, and . . . can this be Rover?" he asked.

Poppy laughed. "The bracelet was a present from Aunt El and Uncle Mike on my ninth birthday, the first year I lived in Providence. They've given me a charm every year since, or Aunt El has since Uncle Mike died. It tells the story of my life."

"But not the whole story."

"What do you mean?" Poppy asked.

"I mean it leaves out the first eight years. What happened during the years before you came to Providence? I'd really like to know."

Her response was automatic. She stiffened and tried to pull away, but Josh held on tight.

"That was a long time ago. I don't like to talk about it," she said. She couldn't have put more distance between them if she had gotten up and walked to the other side of the room.

Abruptly, Josh let her go. "Damn it, Poppy. Whenever I mention your past, you slam the door between us. I don't just want your body. I want to know all of you."

Released from the protection of Josh's arms, Poppy felt small and alone. Like she was six years old again.

"Mama was killed in a car accident," she began in a hushed tone. "She was beautiful, much prettier than me, and so sweet. Men took advantage of her. I tried to protect her but in the end I couldn't. She went to heaven and I landed in a foster home.

"The other children came and went, back to their parents, to relatives or other homes, but I stayed for two years. The couple who took me in—I can't bring myself to call them parents—liked having me around to take care of the younger kids. I was always old for my age. I think I'd have died of grief and loneliness if it hadn't been for the other children."

"And your father?" Josh asked quietly.

"He abandoned Mama before I was born. Mama left home when she was sixteen and had me not long after. I don't have many clear memories of those early years. Just a lot of old apartments in new towns. It seemed like we were always 'getting a fresh start.'

"When I think about it now, I don't know how she did it. Supported a baby when she wasn't much more than a baby herself. But she wouldn't give me up. She loved me, and I know she did the best she could."

Josh was silent for a moment, absorbing what she had said. He finally understood the vulnerability he'd sensed beneath the surface of this strong, vibrant woman. He wanted so much to take the frightened little girl in his arms and comfort her. But what right did he have?

Poppy's words burned in his brain. *He abandoned Mama before I was born.* If he started an affair with Poppy and then left, would he be any better than her father? As much as he wanted the woman, he couldn't risk hurting the child again. He cared for both of them too much.

Josh took Poppy's hands and helped her to her feet. Gone was any hint of the passion they had shared moments earlier. He hugged her as gently as if she were one of his nieces. "Thank you, Poppy," he murmured into her hair. "Thank you for telling me. I think I'd better go now. We both have an early morning."

As suddenly as he'd appeared in her garden that afternoon, he was gone.

Chapter Six

Forty feet up a rickety wooden ladder, Poppy felt her anger and humiliation blaze as brightly as the noonday sun. She sat just outside a shaft of sunlight that marked the entrance to the lava tube, hugging her knees in the cool darkness.

Step into my parlor and I'll share my innermost secrets and desires. If only she'd known her bantering comment would come true, Poppy thought bitterly. She should never have let Josh talk her into revealing her past. A trickster, that's what he was. More like a coyote than the rattlesnake she first compared him to. Grinning and devious, he was ready to take advantage at the first sign of vulnerability.

And he had the nerve to act so sanctimonious about it. As if he were doing her a favor by running out, just when she most needed his understanding and acceptance. She wondered how many times he'd run away when the intimacy became too much for him.

Poppy rose and dusted the seat of her hiking shorts. *I can't sit here all day feeling sorry for myself*, she thought. *Might as well look around.*

She made her way carefully through the darkness, shining her flashlight against the walls of the subterranean cavern created millions of years ago by once-active volcanos. The inner cores of their lava flows had cooled more quickly than the outer crust, forming this network of caverns and tunnels. Uncle Mike said it was like the hole in a donut dropped into boiling grease.

Poppy smiled at the memory. She and Mike had explored this lava tube in the Cinder Cones region of the East Mojave when she was a teenager. Not much had changed since then. In fact, she'd be willing to bet that was the same old ladder they'd descended almost a decade ago.

Poppy wound her way through the first tunnel, stooping as the passageway constricted. Up ahead, she saw another shaft of sunlight like the one created by the hole she'd come through. If she wasn't mistaken, the great cave was off to the left.

The beam of Poppy's flashlight danced over the walls of the cavern. Ah, just as she remembered. There was an opening at the bottom of the west wall. She lay on the cave floor and shone her light through a narrow passage into the vast darkness beyond.

She hesitated for just a moment. It might be a little spooky in there without Uncle Mike to keep her company. Still, she wasn't ready to climb back up into the sunshine and face Josh again. She'd done her best to ignore him all morning. When he attempted to draw her into conversation, she'd replied as briefly as possible. She was sure Meg and Carlos hadn't missed the hurt and anger in her voice. She'd never been good at hiding her feelings.

After lunch, Josh retreated to his camper. Meg had given her a sympathetic hug and insisted on doing the cleanup while Poppy took the afternoon off. She was tired but much too agitated to take a nap. So she'd grabbed her backpack, flashlight, and canteen and headed for the lava tube, calling out to Meg that she was going for a walk.

All in all, it had been a miserable morning. *I'll take my chances down here with the bats*, Poppy thought. *At least I know what to expect from them.*

She flattened herself against the rock and wriggled through the narrow opening, pushing the backpack in front of her.

"Hello," she called.

"Hello, hello, hello," the cave echoed back.

Poppy smiled. Instead of being eerie, the great cave seemed like an old friend, still dear and familiar after a long separation.

"How you been?" Poppy called.

"You been, been, been?" the cave answered.

Overhead, Poppy heard the flapping of wings. "Shhh, you're scaring the bats!" she whispered, and then giggled, not sure if she was addressing herself or the echo.

Training her light on the floor so as not to disturb the little mammals roosting above, Poppy began a slow trek around the the vast underground room. The light from the opening she'd just crawled through provided a murky subterranean glow in this end of the cave. As she progressed farther along the cavern wall the glow faded to almost total darkness. Poppy switched off her flashlight for a moment and let the cool, damp atmosphere envelop her. It was strangely peaceful, like being deep under the sea.

Suddenly, from just under her feet, she heard a low, rasping hiss. She jumped backwards, banging her shoulder against the cave wall. The flashlight flew out of her hand and landed on the lava floor.

Could a snake have fallen through the entrance and crawled all the way back here? she wondered. It sure sounded like one. Poppy gathered her courage. On hands and knees, she groped tentatively around her in the darkness, hoping not to encounter a cold reptilian body.

Ah! Her fingertips brushed the hard rubberized surface of the flashlight. *Dear God, don't let it be broken*, Poppy prayed. She flipped the switch and a strong beam of light cut through the gloom.

A fledgling barn owl seemed paralyzed by the sudden brightness. But only for a moment. He emitted a series of loud rasping hisses while bobbing his head like a punchdrunk prizefighter trying to avoid a blow. Although his wings were partially feathered, the little bird's body was still covered with snowy fluff. A huge beak dominated his quizzical heart-shaped face.

The sight of the comical little bird trying his best to intimidate her was too much for Poppy. Whether from humor, relief, or the tangled emotions that had brought her to the lava tube, she wasn't sure, but her knees suddenly felt as rubbery as week-old gelatin. She abruptly sat on the cavern floor and laughed until she cried.

"You sure gave me a scare," she said, wiping tears from her eyes. "But I bet I'm not nearly as scared as you are."

Just learning to fly, she guessed. She trained the light to the left of the little bird, being careful not to blind him. He seemed unhurt. He must have fallen from his home, up above someplace on the cave wall. He'd managed to flutter down but didn't have the strength or courage to fly back up. He obviously couldn't fend for himself yet.

Poppy shone her light on the volcanic walls of the great cave. Yep, there it was, a long, narrow ledge about twenty-five feet up.

In addition to being the only members of the owl family who hissed instead of hooting, barn owls also didn't believe in building nests, she recalled. They deposited their eggs in abandoned buildings, barns, tree cavities, mine shafts, or in this case, on a convenient ledge in a lava tube.

Convenient if you're an owl, Poppy thought wryly. Still, it didn't look like a hard climb. The walls sloped gently up until about the last ten feet. And there were plenty of finger and toe holds. She'd scaled much steeper cliffs than this one, growing up in the East Mojave. Aunt El always swore she was part bighorn sheep.

Now if she could only catch the little guy. Poppy circled around the fledgling, getting as close as she dared. She turned the light off for a slow count of one hundred and then shone it right in his face.

"Gotcha!" She pounced, covering the startled bird with her open backpack. Quickly but carefully, she upended the pack and zipped it almost shut, leaving a small space for air.

The fledgling's struggles lasted only a few moments. He seemed disoriented or perhaps just worn out by his ordeal.

"Now to get you home," Poppy said. She donned the pack and started her ascent.

The first part was easy, even with a flashlight in one hand. She stopped for a minute, resting her face against the cool canyon wall before starting the harder second stage of her climb.

"It's okay, baby," she cooed. "We're almost there."

Carefully, she found a finger hold in the rock and began to work her way up. Anchor three limbs before moving the fourth, she told herself. Uncle Mike had drilled the old climbers' axiom into her years ago. What would he say about her making this climb alone, in the dark?

Better not to think about that, Poppy decided, feeling a little guilty. After all, she was a grown woman now and quite capable of taking care of herself. Even if some people insisted on treating her like a child.

Keeping the flashlight in her left hand, she made slow but steady progress. Finally her fingertips touched the ledge.

"We made it, baby. Whew, that was a little scarier than I expected." Poppy perched on the edge of the ledge, trying not to squash the little owl against the wall behind her. He had begun to rustle around, as if he knew he was close to home.

"Hang on for just a few more minutes," Poppy pleaded. She shined her light carefully toward the far end of the ledge. Two owlets blinked in surprise, but mama was nowhere in sight.

"Okay, the coast is clear." As Poppy crawled forward, the little owl in her backpack became increasingly agitated. He flapped his wings, emitting a series of shrill, rasping hisses.

The owlets in the nest answered him with raucous hisses of their own. Soon the huge empty space echoed with a cacophony of angry, frightened owl noises.

Poppy kept her right shoulder pressed firmly against

the canyon wall. Just a few more feet. Then she could open her pack and let the little guy out.

"HSSSSSS! HSSSSS!" That was no baby! She threw herself down on the ledge as a rush of air passed within inches of her head. The flashlight clattered to the floor below. With a final bang, it hit bottom. The light went out.

"Stay calm," Poppy told herself. She quickly shrugged off the backpack, unzipped it, and placed it on the ledge in front of her. Crouching, she scrambled backwards, putting as much distance as possible between herself and the angry mother owl.

When she had moved as close to the opposite end of the ledge as she dared, Poppy sat and put her head between her knees, her arms crossed overhead. She remained very still and prayed mama owl would be satisfied with the return of her baby. She knew barn owls were not normally aggressive, but even the little robins in her backyard dive-bombed anyone who approached too close to their nest. A parent's instinct to protect its young was as old as life itself.

After what seemed like an eternity, Poppy dared to raise her head. The hissing, scrabbling noises at the other end of the ledge had quieted. She guessed the mother owl had rejoined her babies. She took several deep breaths and tried to still her racing pulse. It looked like she might be here awhile. Climbing down without a light was out of the question.

This is a fine mess you've gotten yourself into, Poppy Sullivan, she thought. She'd been so proud, so sure of her ability to return the fledgling to his perch. But she'd forgotten the first rule of desert travel. *Always tell someone where you're going and when they can expect you to return.* Meg may have seen which direction she headed in, but Poppy doubted Josh and crew even knew the lava tube existed. It wasn't on any maps of the preserve.

Darn Josh O'Donnell. *If he hadn't gotten me so upset I wouldn't have behaved like such a fool*, she thought.

But you should have known better, a little voice whispered.

All right, Jiminy Cricket, she grumbled inwardly. Pride got me up on this ledge. Now pride will have to keep me company. At least I brought my canteen, she thought, giving the canvas-covered receptacle at her belt a reassuring pat. I won't die of thirst before someone finds me.

If they find you, the voice said.

Poppy felt her stomach knot with fear. She couldn't, wouldn't give in to panic. Far below, she could see a dim glow at the entrance to the great cave. It was a beacon of hope in the darkness. She made herself as comfortable as possible against the unforgiving rock wall and settled in for a long wait.

What's wrong with me? Josh wondered. He sprawled on his bunk in the camper, staring at the ceiling. He had been unable to concentrate on the dozen things he

needed to accomplish before returning to the field for
the late afternoon shoot.

He thought he'd done the right thing by leaving Poppy
last night. God knows it hadn't been easy. So why was
he feeling like a miserable, lowdown, lying dog?

His past relationships hadn't been so difficult or
confusing. Sure, they'd ended in regret, sadness,
occasionally even anger. But he hadn't felt guilty
because he'd been honest from the very beginning. Or
had he?

Was it possible that he used his nomadic lifestyle as
an excuse to avoid commitment? He'd cared for the
women in his past, but when it came time to pack up
and move on, he hadn't invited them to come along.

No, that would have meant allowing another human
being to penetrate the protective shell he crawled into
years ago, when his parents divorced. He'd learned at
the tender age of thirteen that relationships don't last,
and he never wanted to experience that pain again. No
woman had been important enough to risk loving in the
old-fashioned way, the way that promised "until death
do us part."

Until now, he thought. *Until Poppy.*

No wonder she was angry and upset. He had asked,
no, insisted that she allow him into her confidence. She
shared the most painful memories of her childhood.
Then he walked out. No matter what his intentions, it
must have felt like a rejection to Poppy.

Josh cursed himself for being an insensitive, hypocritical fool. He had wounded the person he cared most about in the world. The woman he was falling in love with.

The thought brought Josh bolt upright on the bunk. Was he in love with Poppy? Really in love for the first time in his life? He felt as if someone had knocked the wind out of him. Whether it was love, or lust, or some strange desert enchantment he was experiencing, he didn't know for sure. He could sort all that out later. Right now, he had to find Poppy and apologize.

Josh opened the door of his camper to see Rover parked on the dirt road just beyond their campsite. Meg stood atop a red-black volcanic formation, peering through binoculars.

"What's up?" Josh called as he approached her. "Where's Poppy?" Even as the words left his mouth, Josh had a gut feeling that something was wrong. Meg's worried expression when she lowered the binoculars confirmed his suspicion.

"I wish I knew," Meg replied. "She took off walking about two hours ago and I haven't seen her since. I was just about to come and get you."

"Why didn't you tell me sooner?" Josh demanded.

"I'm sorry. Maybe I should have. It's just that she seemed upset. I thought she might need a little time alone."

"No, I'm sorry," Josh replied. "Poppy and I had a misunderstanding. It's my fault she's upset. I shouldn't have barked at you."

"No problem, boss." Meg patted his shoulder. "Do you think we should organize a search party?"

"Here's the map." Carlos joined them in his usual quiet fashion.

Josh glanced at the lowering sun and then at his watch. Four PM. The sun would set about six o'clock. That gave them two hours of daylight. Poppy wouldn't die of exposure this time of year, but if she was lying out there hurt, or had been bitten by a rattlesnake . . . Josh felt the blood drain from his face.

He took the map from Carlos, barely able to hold it in his trembling hands. "Thank you, amigo," he said.

With great effort, Josh took charge of his emotions. He couldn't afford to think about all the terrible things that might have happened. He shook out the map and concentrated on the task at hand.

"When Poppy left, which direction did she go?"

"Due north," Meg answered.

"It looks like she was headed for Cow Cove, although she could have taken this dirt road and circled back to Aiken Wash." Josh traced a broken line on the map connecting Interstate 15 to Aiken Mine Road and the wash.

"That's where I'll look," Meg volunteered. "A stream runs through the wash and there are lots of tall green willow trees. I'll bet Poppy's sitting under one of them right now, wiggling her toes in the water."

"I hope you're right, Meg. Carlos, why don't you check Cow Cove. I'll take the Cinder Cones area. We'll each need to carry extra water, flares, and a first aid kit, just in case Poppy's been hurt. If she can't be moved, send up a flare and we'll find you."

Carlos bobbed his head. "I go right now." He hurried off to collect the necessary supplies.

"I assume she took some water," Josh said, shooting a questioning glance at Meg.

"She had her canteen and a backpack," Meg replied. "One more thing. I know this sounds strange, but I could have sworn she was carrying a flashlight."

Josh thought about Meg's last remark as he hiked quickly over the red-black landscape. It was their only real clue to her whereabouts. The Cinder Cones covered over 25,000 acres, he recalled from guidebooks he'd read about the area. The desolate geography heightened Josh's anxiety. He felt as if he were hiking across the surface of the moon.

Josh stopped again to check his watch and compass. If his calculations were right, he should be there soon.

He moved more slowly now, crisscrossing the rocky terrain, keeping his eyes trained downward. Finally he saw a gaping hole in the volcanic crust. Beside it, on a small sign close to ground level, were the stenciled words LAVA TUBE.

Josh felt a surge of relief. He knew Poppy was inside. He could almost feel her energy radiating up through the earth. Now he just had to find her and tell her what a jerk he'd been. Tell her he cared for her and wanted . . . wanted what? He wasn't sure. The feelings were too new, his emotions raw. For right now, it would be enough to hold her in his arms and know she was safe.

It had taken him less than an hour to find the lava tube. With any luck, they could be back to camp before dark. Josh wouldn't allow himself to consider the possibility that Poppy might be seriously hurt, but he knew something had gone wrong. She wouldn't have intentionally stayed away this long.

Josh climbed down the rickety ladder to the cavern floor. He stood still for a minute, allowing his eyes to adjust to the dim interior.

"Poppy?" he called, sweeping the cavern with the powerful beam of his lantern. He received no response except for the high-pitched squeaks of bats disturbed by the light.

Josh wound his way through the tunnel, pausing occasionally to call Poppy's name. He didn't really expect an answer. No sound could escape the confines of the solid lava walls.

He muttered a curse as he bumped into a low spot in the ceiling, stopping momentarily to rub the goose egg rising on his forehead. If he didn't slow down, Meg and Carlos would have to rescue him.

Finally he saw light. The tunnel widened into a room like the first one, partially illuminated by a shaft of sunlight. Josh eagerly searched the far recesses of the cavern with his lantern. It was empty. And as far as he could see, the tube ended here.

He'd been so sure he would find Poppy. All his pent-up fear, anxiety, and frustration exploded in two words: "Damn it!"

"Josh?" The voice was slightly tremulous but hopeful. Nothing had ever sounded so sweet.

"Poppy, Poppy darling, where are you?"

"Look down," she called. "Close to the ground. You'll see the entrance."

"Hang on, sweetheart. I'm coming," Josh literally dove into the opening. He wriggled through within seconds, heedless of the abrasions to his knees and elbows as he scraped over the rough volcanic rock.

He emerged in an enormous underground cavern, much larger than the first two he'd entered. Again he searched the area with his lantern. Again no sign of Poppy.

"Okay, I give up," he said, attempting to keep his tone light. "Where are you?"

"Look up."

There, on a narrow ledge twenty-five feet above the floor, her hair askew and clothing smeared with what appeared to be bird droppings, sat Poppy Sullivan, the love of his life.

Chapter Seven

"**A**re you all right?" Josh asked.

"I'd be a lot better if you'd shine that light someplace else." Poppy raised an arm to shield her eyes. Now she understood how the fledgling owl felt. Three hours in almost total darkness made you very light-sensitive.

"What in the heck are you doing up there?"

"Rescuing baby owls. Can we save the questions for later? I'd really like to get off this ledge."

"Your wish is my command. I don't get many chances to save a damsel in distress."

Always with the glib reply, she thought. No matter. She was bone-weary, hungry, and so glad to see Josh that she was almost ready to forgive him. Almost.

"I hope you brought along an extra flashlight," she said.

"I did. And water and a first aid kit. Heck, I might even be able to conjure up a candy bar."

Poppy watched the beam from Josh's lantern move swiftly up the lower portion of the cave wall. "Watch out for low-flying owls."

"Owls, dragons, makes no difference." Josh sounded slightly winded from his rapid ascent. He'd reached the steepest part of the climb now. "Sir Josh O'Donnell . . . always gets his damsel."

Poppy giggled in the darkness above. "Methinks you're mixing your metaphors, Sir Josh."

"Mixing metaphors is my specialty. In fact, it's probably what I do best. Other than rescuing fair maidens, of course." Josh's head appeared atop the ledge. "Nice place you have here." He shined the light toward the far end of Poppy's temporary refuge, where the owls resumed their rasping, hissing clamor. "Noisy neighbors, though."

"No kidding." Poppy waited as Josh pulled himself up beside her. She couldn't see him clearly, but she sensed his closeness. And then suddenly she was in his arms. Josh's hands stroked her face, brushing the hair back from her forehead.

Poppy gasped in surprise. She half-turned to face him, a protest on her lips. Before she could find any words, he crushed her to his chest. She felt his lips brush her hair.

"Poppy, Poppy. I was so worried. Are you sure you're all right?" Josh asked. There was an unfamiliar hoarseness in his voice.

"I'm fine. Really." Poppy squeaked. She had been fine. Right up until the moment Josh embraced her. Then she'd experienced a sweet, melting sensation. Like warm chocolate, she thought.

Was it possible that Josh really cared for her? No, she couldn't believe it. He was carried away by the emotion of the moment. Of course he'd been worried. Maybe he even felt responsible. But he couldn't be trusted. *When I needed him, he ran away,* she reminded herself sternly.

She pulled free of his embrace. "Can we go now? I'm sure Meg and Carlos are worried. And I could really use a hot bath."

"Yeah, sure. I'm sorry. I guess I wanted to . . . I mean, I was so darn glad to see you. I shouldn't have grabbed you like that."

"It's okay," Poppy said. "Let's just get out of here."

They hiked back in silence. The red-orange sunset cast an eerie glow over the volcanic landscape.

How could he have been such a idiot? He'd lunged at Poppy like some kind of Neanderthal. All the repressed fear of the afternoon and his elation at finding her had finally boiled over. He'd acted without thinking. But that was part of the problem, wasn't it? Once again, he hadn't considered her feelings. No wonder she'd pushed him away.

If he was going to talk to her, he'd better do it soon. In a few minutes they'd be back at camp. He had to return to Los Angeles after tomorrow's shoot to meet with Mother Nature's Workshop, the educational film company bankrolling his documentary. This was his last chance to set things right with Poppy. He had to at least try.

"How did you find me?" Poppy asked.

The question provided Josh with the opening he'd hoped for. "I called Brad on the cell phone and asked where you might be going with a flashlight in the middle of the day." At least she was speaking to him. That was probably more than he deserved.

"Meg told you I took a flashlight with me," Poppy guessed.

Josh nodded. "That gal doesn't miss much."

"I know you all must have been worried. I'm sorry I caused so much trouble."

Josh stopped and took Poppy by the shoulders. As the sun slipped slowly toward the horizon, the sky took on more vivid colors. Poppy was outlined in red, orange, purple, and violet. A slight breeze ruffled her hair, which, as usual, was escaping in every direction. How could a woman who'd spend the afternoon in a lava tube manage to look so appealing?

He gently took her hands. "No, I'm the one who's sorry. I'm sorry I grabbed you without any consideration for your feelings. And I'm even sorrier for my behavior last night. I know how difficult it must have been for you to share your childhood memories. It took a lot of courage. I shouldn't have run out on you."

"Listen, it's okay. No big deal." Poppy pulled her

hands free and took a couple of steps in the direction of camp.

"No, Poppy, it's not okay."

She stopped and turned toward him, her expression a mixture of sympathy and distrust.

Josh forged ahead. "I've spent most of my life running from commitment and the pain I associated with it. Good old Josh, always ready with a joke or a tall tale. Just don't try to pin him down.

"The truth is, Poppy, I've been afraid to let anyone get close to me. I didn't want to give anyone the power to hurt me. Until now."

He made no attempt to touch her, but locked her in his gaze. "I care about you, Poppy. More than I've ever cared for any woman. I don't expect you to forgive my insensitive and cowardly behavior, but I would like another chance."

Poppy took a full step backwards. Josh always managed to disarm her. Just when she thought she had him figured out, he hit her with another surprise. He said he cared for her. What exactly did those words mean to a man like Josh O'Donnell?

In all honesty, Poppy had to admit that she, too, feared commitment. She loved children and animals without reservation. But in relationships with men, she'd been much more cautious. She couldn't forget what her mother's sweetness and vulnerability had cost them both.

Somehow Josh had slipped past her defenses. He'd made her want to share her joys and sorrows, her hopes for the future, and even the pain of her past. Looking at him now, so sincere and repentant, she felt her anger fade with the last rays of the sun.

"I know you were trying to protect me," she said. "But I'm not seven years old anymore. I needed your friendship and acceptance last night. I didn't need to be treated like a child."

Poppy took a deep breath and continued. "I appreciate your honesty, Josh. I really do. I'm just not sure there's any future in this relationship for either of us."

She knew she spoke the truth. Surely Josh must realize it too. So why did it hurt so much to say it?

The pain Poppy felt was reflected on Josh's handsome face. "I understand," he said, shouldering his backpack. "And you're probably right. I have to go back to L.A. for a few days on business. I'll be leaving tomorrow afternoon. Please, think it over. And if you change your mind, just whistle." Josh winked an amber eye and turned toward camp.

Trailing slightly behind him, Poppy wasn't sure if the dampness on his cheek was real or another illusion of the East Mojave twilight.

"There they are!" The shout rang out in the cool desert air. Meg came running up and enveloped her friend in a bear hug. "Hey, you're shivering!" she exclaimed. "Didn't this big oaf think to bring a jacket?"

"I wasn't cold until just now," Poppy protested through lips compressed to keep her teeth from chattering.

Meg put a protective arm around her shoulders. "Come on, honey. Let's get you warmed up by the fire. I bet you're hungry, too."

Josh watched helplessly as Meg led Poppy away. For the second time that day, he cursed himself for being an insensitive fool. Why hadn't he offered Poppy the blanket he carried in his pack? Or at least given her a candy bar? Some rescuer he was. He couldn't seem to do anything right. In all his travels, he'd never felt so out of his element. Love, it seemed, was an uncharted territory.

"I'll get a jacket," he mumbled, and retreated in the direction of his camper.

"Senorita Poppy, you are okay . . . yes?" Carlos appeared at her elbow, his expression concerned.

"I'm fine." She gave him a quick hug. "I'm so sorry to have worried all of you. Did anyone call Aunt El?"

"We were waiting to see if you got back before dark. We didn't want to frighten her." Before Meg finished speaking, the powerful headlights of a Park Service truck illuminated the campsite. Brad climbed out and loped toward them.

"Boy, am I glad to see you!" he said. "What happened? Are you all right?"

"It's a long story, but I'm fine. Would you be a dear and call Aunt El for me? You can borrow Josh's cell phone. He'll fill you in on the details."

Within minutes, Poppy was seated before a roaring blaze, eating an impromptu meal of canned vegetable soup, soda crackers, sliced apples, and cheese. She was wrapped in the same Pendleton shirt she'd borrowed from Josh the night they met. The scent of his bay rum aftershave clung to the fabric, mingling deliciously with the fragrance of mesquite wood emanating from the campfire. Poppy pulled the shirt more closely around her, enjoying its warmth and comfort. She couldn't help wishing the garment's owner had been able to offer the same comfort last night.

Now he was pacing back and forth in front of the fire. Every few minutes, he crossed to Poppy and stared at her, as if to reassure himself that she was really all right. Carlos kept the flames stoked. Meg and Brad hovered close, ready to refill her cup or plate. Finally she couldn't stand it any longer.

"Okay, you guys. I spent the afternoon on a ledge with a family of owls. I didn't break any bones, or get snake bit, or struck by lightning. In fact, when I wash off the rest of this owl poop, I'll be the same old Poppy who drove up here this morning. So quit treating me like I'm going to break, will you?"

The four exchanged surprised glances and then burst out laughing.

"Yep, it's the same old Poppy," Brad said.

"Girl, you had us so worried!" Meg exclaimed.

"I know, I know. It was a really dumb thing to do, going off without telling anybody. Then when I saw that baby owl on the cavern floor, well, I couldn't just leave him."

"Like you couldn't leave the skunk kitten whose den was flooded. She turned out to be a female who came back every year to have her litters under the front porch of the cafe," Brad said.

Poppy leapt to the defense. "She was actually very well-behaved. The only person she ever sprayed was Billy Preston and that was because he poked a stick under the porch."

"It didn't do much for the cafe's business that week." Brad's guffaw was infectious. Encouraged by the others' response, he went on. "And then there was the time she rescued a stray dog who'd been hit on the highway. Both its back legs were broken. I'll be darned if she didn't teach that little dog to walk on its front legs with its hind end up in the air. It was the funniest looking thing you ever saw. But any kid who cracked a smile risked getting a thrashing from Poppy."

"Toodles was a courageous little animal and I happen to know it hurt her feelings when people laughed at her," Poppy said.

"Then there was the gopher snake who curled up in Uncle Mike's boot one cold morning and the kit fox who . . ."

"All right, Brad. I think we all get the picture. I have a soft spot for animals and kids and big dumb lummoxes in Park Service uniforms. But don't think I couldn't still put you in your place if I wanted to."

Poppy tried to glare threateningly at her old friend, but a smile tugged at her lips, ruining the effect.

The park ranger held up his hands in mock surrender. "I'll say no more."

"Now, I think I better start home before it gets any later," Poppy said, rising reluctantly. The food, fire, and genial company made the long drive ahead of her seem almost unbearable.

"No need for that," Meg said. "I asked Brad to tell Aunt El you'd be bunking with me tonight. I hope you don't mind. I have an extra bed with clean sheets and a full tank of water for the shower."

"But what about meals for tomorrow?" Poppy asked.

Brad spoke up. "I have the day off, so I volunteered to be the delivery man. I'll drop off the ice chests and other gear at the cafe tonight, then pick them up again in the morning. Of course, I'll be well paid for my efforts." Brad rubbed his ample midsection in exaggerated anticipation.

"Thank you, Brad." Poppy rose on her tiptoes to give the big man a kiss on the cheek. "I guess I am a little tired. Good night, all."

Her eyes briefly met Josh's as she headed for Meg's camper. He had been quiet all evening, barely smiling at Brad's stories while the others roared with laughter. She couldn't quite read the look in his eyes. Was it relief? Hope? Uncertainty? Or could it be love?

Poppy didn't want to think about that possibility. She

was suddenly exhausted from the day's events. Maybe tomorrow things would be clearer. Right now, all she wanted was the warm shower and clean sheets Meg had promised.

Later, sitting at the camper's small table with a towel wrapped around her damp hair, Poppy felt almost human again. Meg had loaned her some flannel pajamas and an old terry cloth robe. The bathroom door opened and her friend's freshly scrubbed face appeared in a cloud of rose-scented steam.

"How about some camomile tea?" Meg asked.

"That sounds wonderful." Poppy spotted a stainless steel teapot on the stove behind her. "I'll put the water on while you finish up."

The teapot was just starting to whistle when Meg joined her, wearing a soft, faded sweatsuit, her face wreathed with pink curlers. "That warm shower felt great. It's amazing how chilly it gets around here when the sun goes down."

"I've always been especially sensitive to the cold," Poppy confessed. "The slightest little breeze sends me running for a sweater. Comes from growing up in the desert, I guess."

"Have you lived here all your life?" Meg set a steaming cup of tea in front of her.

"No." Poppy fiddled with her teabag, overcome by her old reluctance. Meg had been very kind to her. There was really no reason to hide her past, no threat from the affable redhead who had become her friend. "You know that I was adopted?"

"Yes, but I thought maybe your biological parents lived around here. I'm sorry. I didn't mean to pry. We don't have to talk about it if you don't want to."

"No, it's okay. I was raised by a single mom. She was killed in a car accident when I was six. Then I lived in a foster home for a couple of years before Aunt El and Uncle Mike adopted me. It was a real hard time for me. The couple who took me at first were only interested in the money. I think if it hadn't been for the other children, especially the little ones who loved me and let me love them back, I wouldn't have survived."

"I'm so sorry." Meg reached across the table and squeezed Poppy's hand.

As she sipped the hot, calming tea, Poppy remembered the nightmares she'd had for years after coming to the East Mojave. In her dreams, Aunt El and Uncle Mike disappeared or died or moved away from Providence and she was sent back to the foster home. How many nights had Aunt El gotten up and rocked her in the big oak chair? Long after she was much too big for rocking, she'd sit in her adopted mom's lap, thin legs dangling close to the floor, as Aunt El rocked and crooned a tuneless Irish lullaby. Eventually, the dreams had come less frequently and finally they stopped completely.

"Have you told Josh about your childhood?"

The question startled Poppy out of her reverie. Her lips formed an ironic smile. "Last night. He couldn't get out of the house fast enough."

"Ah. That's why you were upset," Meg said.

Poppy nodded. "He apologized today. He seemed so sincere that I couldn't stay angry." She hesitated for a moment and then added, "I guess it's no secret that we're attracted to each other."

Meg said nothing, but her eyes twinkled over the top of her teacup.

Poppy plunged ahead. "I know Josh means well. I'm just not sure he's capable of making a long-term commitment to anyone."

Meg was silent, apparently lost in thought. Outside, crickets chirped and small creatures rustled in the night. "Have you noticed that Carlos has an unusual accent?" she asked finally, setting down her cup.

Poppy was thrown off-balance by the sudden change of subject. "I have. I didn't want to ask because I thought it might embarrass him."

"Carlos is from the Yucatan Peninsula in Mexico. His mother is a full-blooded Maya Indian and his father is a mixture of Spanish and Indian. His first language was the Mayan Kanjobal. Josh met Carlos when he was filming a documentary about the animals that live around the ruins of ancient Mayan temples. When the tourists go home from Chichen Itza and Toulum and some of the lesser-known archeological sites, the night life gets pretty wild.

"Anyway, Carlos wasn't much more than a kid. He

hung around all the time, watching everything with those big brown eyes of his. Josh took a real shine to him. He started giving Carlos simple jobs to do and found that he was quick and eager. When Josh left the Yucatan, he took Carlos with him."

"But what about his family?" Poppy asked. "And his schooling? It sounds like he was a little young to go traipsing around the world with Josh."

"Josh arranged for Carlos to stay with his sister, Elaine, for the first few years. He hired a tutor until Carlos was fluent enough in English to attend high school and paid for his board and keep. Not that Elaine minded having him. She'd just gone through a nasty divorce and was trying to work and raise the three girls by herself. Carlos was a godsend. He helped Elaine with the housework and the girls and they became a second family to him."

"How could his real family let him go?" Poppy wondered aloud.

"I'm sure Carlos' parents saw it as an opportunity for their son to have a better life. He goes home several times a year, and with the money he's made working for Josh, he's been able to help support his younger brothers and sister."

"How long have he and Josh been together?"

"Let's see. Carlos couldn't have been more than fourteen when Josh first met him. Last year, when he turned twenty-one, Josh sponsored him for citizenship. Must be seven, eight years, at least."

Suddenly it dawned on Poppy what Meg was trying to tell her. "I guess that's a pretty long-term commitment, isn't it?"

Meg grinned as she picked up her cup. "It sure is."

Poppy rolled over in the narrow bunk and stretched luxuriously. Morning sunlight poured through the camper window. Outside she heard the crunch of boots on gravel.

Crimeny! she thought, fumbling for her watch. How late had she slept?

Eight-thirty. The crew would be coming in for breakfast soon. Poppy pulled on the jeans and flannel shirt Meg had laid out for her. Cinched tightly around the waist, the jeans fit well enough. She splashed her face with water and wound her unruly hair into a tight bun.

"Morning, sleepyhead!" Brad's booming baritone greeted her as she stepped out of the camper. "I was beginning to think I'd to have to eat this all by myself."

"No such luck," Poppy said. "In just a few minutes we'll have three hungry mouths to feed. Is there anything I can do?"

"Why don't you sit and have a cup of coffee? I think I'm just about ready for 'em."

Poppy surveyed the loaded camp tables. She had to hand it to Brad. He'd done a good job of setting up. True, he hadn't included all the pretty touches she added to the tables, but Aunt El's food didn't need much embellishment. The ice chests full of hot and cold dishes sat in Rover's open cargo area.

"Thanks, pardner." Poppy filled a blue enamel camp mug half full of coffee, then added almost as much milk. She was reaching for the sugar when a brightly colored flyer in the center of the table caught her eye.

RATTLESNAKE BALL AT THE PROVIDENCE COMMUNITY CENTER. COWBOYS, BELLES, AND LITTLE BUCKEROOS WELCOME. KICK UP YOUR HEELS TO THE SOUNDS OF THE LONELY TRIANGLE BAND. The date mentioned was the upcoming Friday night.

"The spring dance. It can't be the first weekend of April already!" Poppy exclaimed.

"Sure is," Brad replied. "They're a little late with the flyers this year. You plan on attending?"

"I haven't missed one yet."

"Yahoo! We're gonna have ourselves a time." Brad lifted Poppy off the chair and two-stepped her around the campsite.

"Hey, you big oaf," Poppy protested, laughing. "Don't you know you're supposed to ask first?"

"What, and give you a chance to say no? Not on your life." Brad whirled her around a few more times to illustrate his point.

"Is this a private party? Or is everyone invited?" Meg waved a hand in greeting.

Poppy hung on to Brad for a moment to steady herself as she watched the approaching column. Meg was in the lead this morning. She and Carlos wore expectant smiles. Behind them, Josh glowered under his bush hat.

He's jealous. The realization hit Poppy like a warm desert breeze, producing a glow of feminine satisfaction. Although she and Brad joked and flirted, there had never been anything serious between them. She loved Brad like a brother. Josh evidently didn't understand the limits of their relationship.

"Everyone's invited," she said when she could catch her breath. "To the country and western dance at Providence Community Center this Friday night. Brad and I were just warming up."

"It sounds like a blast, but I have a standing date with the two Petes," said Meg.

"How about you, Carlos?"

"I meet my brother at the airport in Los Angeles on Friday. It's his first visit to this country," Carlos said. "I am sorry, Senorita Poppy. I would love to come."

"Me, too," agreed Meg. "You've given me a great idea, though. After P. J. goes to bed, I think I'll put on some romantic music and see if his father and I still remember how to do it. Dance, that is," she added with a mischievous grin.

Josh said nothing as he walked past the laughing, chattering group toward his camper. The bush hat, pulled low over his eyes, couldn't hide the grim set of his lips. He was obviously in no mood to join in their levity.

Poppy watched his retreating back for just a moment.

Should she give him another chance? It was crazy, she knew. Their lives were so different. And yet, she was drawn to him as she had been to no other man.

Perhaps she had judged him too harshly. Anyhow, she couldn't let him go back to Los Angeles thinking she was still angry.

Poppy took a deep breath, put two fingers in her mouth, and blew. Hard. The shrill whistle bounced off red-black rocks, reverberating in the crystal clear morning air.

Josh turned, astonishment sketched on every plane and angle of his face. A delighted grin spread slowly over his tanned countenance as the significance of Poppy's ear-splitting blast sunk in. *If you change your mind, just whistle.*

"How about you, city boy? Think you can rustle up a pair of cowboy boots by Friday? If I'm going to get my toes stomped, I prefer to have it done Western-style."

"Don't you worry none, ma'am," he drawled, removing his battered hat and placing it over his heart. "I'll find me a pair of boots if I have to hold up every store in Los Angeles." Although his tone was bantering, Josh's eyes caressed her with an intimate golden light.

Only four more days until the dance, Poppy thought. An eternity, and yet much too close for comfort.

Chapter Eight

"Who's the hunk?"

The Lonely Triangle had just finished their first set at the Providence Community Center. Rita Mae Evans' question rang out in the silence.

As a ripple of laughter passed through the crowd, Poppy experienced the familiar rush of excitement, the quickening of her pulse. She knew without a particle of doubt which hunk was being referred to.

Rita Mae was right. Uncouth and lecherous, as usual, but right. Even with a dozen pairs of curious eyes trained on her, Poppy couldn't help admiring Josh as he closed the distance between them. A crisp, cream-colored Western shirt complemented his sun-bronzed skin and rich sable hair. Her eyes followed the razor-sharp crease in his jeans past smoothly muscled thighs to a polished but well-worn pair of cowboy boots.

"Hey there, city boy. I was wondering if you'd make it." Poppy was pleased to note her voice sounded quite steady even as a dozen butterflies took flight in her stomach.

Josh stopped in front of her. He seemed different somehow. Subdued, almost tentative. She sensed a vulnerability deep within his amber gaze that she'd never noticed there before.

He answered softly, as though for her ears alone. "Wild horses couldn't keep me away."

Taking his hand, Poppy turned toward the group of young women she'd been chatting with when he arrived. "Let me introduce you around. Rita Mae, Charleen, Betty, this is Josh O'Donnell."

"Pleased to meet you." Josh nodded politely to each of the ladies, seeming oblivious to their admiring glances.

"You're new around here, aren't you?" Rita Mae asked, her syrupy drawl thickened by several cups of spiked punch.

"I've been in the area for a couple of months," Josh replied. "My company is filming a nature documentary in the national preserve."

"My, my. Two whole months. I'm surprised I haven't run into you. My family ranches down at Essex. You plan on doing any filming there?"

"Uh, no. Actually, that's a little outside the boundaries of the preserve."

Rita Mae's greedy gaze slithered down Josh's body. "Too bad. I surely would enjoy showing you around the neighborhood."

Poppy glared at the voluptuous blonde. As usual, Rita Mae had poured herself into jeans that molded every curve. Her fringed western shirt offered a panoramic view of the double-D cleavage that had been her pride and joy since high school. A perky bandana was knotted at her throat.

Poppy clenched her hands at her sides. Oh, how she'd love to pull that bandana just a little tighter, or grab a fistful of those bleached blonde curls. But she wasn't ten years old any more. She wouldn't stoop to throwing Rita Mae down on the dance floor and walloping her, much as she'd love to.

Mercifully, the Lonely Triangle launched into a lively two-step. Poppy shot a withering look at Rita Mae. "Come on, Josh, let's dance."

As she led Josh onto the floor, Poppy heard one of the other women exclaim, "Rita Mae, that was rude."

"Aw, heck, I was just having some fun. Anyhow, I don't see her brand on him."

Poppy looked at Josh and giggled, her anger evaporating. Suddenly, the whole incident seemed pretty silly. "Do you get that reaction from women often?" she asked as he took her in his arms.

"Only the drunk ones."

"I'll bet. You know, they called her Miss Piggy in high school. I can't imagine why." She glanced up at him with innocent blue eyes.

"Oh, now I'm really flattered."

Poppy giggled again and relaxed against him. She felt deliciously light and airy, as if champagne coursed through her veins. Josh maneuvered her expertly through the Western two-step. Three steps forward, two back, turn, turn. "Hey, you're pretty good at this," she said.

"I told you I'm full of surprises."

"Looks like you're wearing a couple of them." Poppy leaned back to peer at his down-at-the-heel footwear. "What's the story behind those boots, city boy? You darn sure didn't buy them yesterday."

"I darn sure didn't." He offered no further explanation but drew her closer as the band switched to a ballad.

Poppy was in no mood to argue. She tucked the question away for later and lifted her arms to encircle Josh's neck. As they swayed together to the mournful strains of Jimmy Rogers, Poppy felt as if all the tiny champagne bubbles inside her had been shaken madly. They were popping and fizzing against the contours of the hard, lean body pressed firmly to hers. She breathed deeply of bay rum aftershave mingled with the intoxicating scent of a young, healthy male.

"Mmmmm. You smell wonderful," she murmured.

"You feel wonderful."

The dance floor was packed, but Poppy barely

noticed. The rest of the world grew hazy and indistinct as she gave herself to the delightful sensations of dancing with Josh.

"Look over there." Josh nodded toward a couple standing at the edge of the crowd. The woman wore a knee-length dress in a soft, shimmering blue that complemented her blue eyes and silver hair. Her escort, a couple of inches shorter, looked handsome in black jeans and a silver Western shirt. As they watched, the man whispered something in his partner's ear. She threw back her head and laughed.

"Aunt El looks lovely, doesn't she?"

"She does indeed. I don't think I've ever seen her look so happy. Who's the gentleman?" Josh asked.

"Homer Bell. He's a retired professor of literature and a poet. They've taken quite a fancy to each other."

Josh brushed Poppy's hair with his lips. "I guess it's never too late to fall in love."

She looked up at him, trying to gauge by his expression if he was teasing. A half-smile twisted his lips but his eyes glowed with amber fire. Was he mocking her? Or himself? His mouth covered hers and everything else faded into insignificance.

She melted against him, savoring the sweetness of his kiss. All around her, elbows found ribs as the residents of the East Mojave whispered about Poppy Sullivan and that filmmaker from Los Angeles. She didn't care. All that mattered was the warmth of his body pressed to hers. While she was wrapped in the sensory cocoon of his embrace, nothing in the world could touch her.

As the last chords of the ballad echoed through the hall, Josh released her. He grinned down at her with that lazy, self-assured smile of his.

He looks a little too pleased with himself, she thought. Like he knew exactly what effect he had on her. Well, she had admirers, too. Plenty of them. She wasn't about to let Josh think she was all marshmallowy over him. Even if it were true. Especially since it was true. She spotted Brad walking toward them.

Trying to appear nonchalant, she turned to Josh. "Look, here's Brad. I promised I'd dance with him."

There was no mistaking the amusement in Josh's eyes now. "I guess I can't expect to monopolize the prettiest girl at the party. Before you go, I want to thank you."

"For the dance?"

Her question went unanswered as the ebullient ranger joined them. As he led Poppy onto the dance floor, she cast an inquiring look over her shoulder.

Josh mouthed the words softly. "For the whistle."

Although Josh was able to claim only a few dances with Poppy, she was rarely out of his sight and never out of his thoughts. He'd spent most of the past week pondering their dilemma. How could a rolling stone and a woman who was so much a part of this enchanted place find happiness together? Or, perhaps more to the point, what did he have to offer? He had learned, painfully, that he could not make decisions for Poppy. She was a strong, independent woman entirely capable of making her own choices.

To further complicate matters, the directors at Mother Nature's Workshop had dealt him an unexpected blow. Due to a cutback in funding, he'd have to trim two weeks off his production schedule. They couldn't have been more enthusiastic about the film clips he'd shown them, or more apologetic about the necessity of reducing his budget. Such were the fiscal realities of public television.

It seemed to Josh that all the forces of business and nature conspired to wrest a decision from him. For once in his life he couldn't walk away from an intimate relationship. Poppy had become too important to him. After several sleepless nights, he'd settled on a plan. It wasn't ideal, he knew. But it was so much more than he'd ever been able to offer before. Now, if he could just get Poppy alone . . .

As the clocked ticked toward midnight, Josh waited for his chance. He danced with Betty and Charlene and quite a few other women whose names he'd forgotten. He even danced with Rita Mae, after she cornered him by the men's room, and had been rewarded with a bruised behind.

Josh had to smile at the mental picture. He must have jumped three feet when Rita Mae pinched him. He debated telling Poppy how the cowgirl had put her brand on him, but decided it probably wasn't a good idea. Besides, they had more important things to discuss tonight.

The Lonely Triangle was taking their final break of the evening. Poppy disengaged herself as tactfully as possible from her partner and headed for the open door. On the way out, she waved at Aunt El, who was chatting with a group of ladies at the refreshment table. Homer stood at her elbow, holding two glasses of punch.

She'd bet a week's register take that Aunt El had had a hand in Homer's new appearance. In his Western duds and shiny black cowboy boots, he looked as much at home at the Rattlesnake Ball as one of the Evans clan. Even from across the room, she could see the spark of pride in his eyes as he watched Aunt El.

Seeing them made her think of Josh's words. *It's never too late to fall in love.* Had Josh guessed? she wondered. He'd have to be blind not to see what the rest of Providence had been talking about for weeks now.

Poppy sighed. Sometimes living in one place for most of your life had its disadvantages. She felt like she'd danced with every male in the East Mojave and fended off questions about Josh from every female.

She'd felt the warmth of his gaze many times during the evening. It seemed as if an invisible thread connected them. Even as she danced with other men, a part of her remained attuned to his presence. Now, without turning, she knew the approaching footsteps belonged to the laughing, golden-eyed stranger who in just a few short weeks had stolen her heart.

"You're losing your touch, O'Donnell. I heard you coming."

"Western boots were not made for stealth."

She leaned against the barn-like structure, enjoying the coolness of the night air against her face. "Which reminds me, I'm still waiting to hear the story behind those boots."

"Come for a drive with me and I'll tell you about the boots and anything else you'd like to know."

"Now that's an offer I can't refuse." Poppy smiled and lightly touched his arm. "Just let me get my wrap."

Josh stood for a moment looking after her. The touch of her hand sent a charge through his body. She was so sweet and so darn desirable. He seemed to lose all control when she was close. But tonight he couldn't let his emotions get away from him. Tonight they needed to talk.

Josh navigated his vehicle slowly past knots of partygoers. He felt a surge of pride when he saw Poppy waiting in front of the community center. She was wrapped in a fringed shawl like those worn by the women of Mexico and Central America. The yellow light over the entrance enveloped her in a soft preternatural glow. He jumped out to open the door.

"Nice wheels," she said. The bright red jeep was an older model, but obviously in mint condition and polished to a high gloss. "This can't be the same jeep you were driving when I met you?"

"The very same. The old girl was a college graduation present from my dad. I haven't been home enough to put many miles on her."

And does the old girl have a name?"

"Actually, no. Do you have any suggestions?" The jeep's tires dug in and kicked up gravel as Josh accelerated onto Lanfair Road.

"Let me think about it. In the meantime, you can tell me how you put all those miles on your boots."

Josh chuckled. It felt so right to have Poppy beside him as they drove down the desert highway, their headlights tracing a path through the moonless night. If only they could have a hundred, a thousand more nights like this one.

"Once upon a time," he began, "there was a very shy and awkward thirteen-year-old boy. His elbows stuck out at right angles from his body, his nose was too big for his face, and he always seemed to be tripping over his own feet. He was surly and secretive and his bony shoulders were hunched with resentment. Although he was an extremely ugly duckling, his mother loved him, as only a mother could, and decided that what he really needed was dance lessons."

"*Dance* lessons?"

Josh chuckled. "You got it. Elaine was taking ballet but there was no way Mom was going to talk me into wearing those tights. So she bought me my first pair of cowboy boots and signed me up for a Western dance class at the same studio. She had to drag me to the first few lessons, and then I only went after she and Elaine swore by everything holy they would never tell my friends.

"You know, although it was years before I admitted it, I really enjoyed those classes. They helped me feel more comfortable with my body, and I discovered it wasn't such a bad thing to be one of the few males in a class full of teenage girls. Being popular was a whole new experience for me."

"Funny, I can't imagine you ever being an ugly duckling. I'll bet even back then the little girls thought you were cute," Poppy said.

Josh reflected on this for a moment. "I think the problem was more with my insides than my outside. I couldn't have been much homelier than most other thirteen-year-olds but I was just plain miserable. I hated school. I hated my life. And most of all, I hated myself."

"That was about the time your mom and dad divorced, wasn't it?"

Josh nodded, his concentration on the road. The pavement had just ended. If memory served him, the turn he wanted should be dead ahead.

"Hang on." The jeep bucked and jolted as he swung onto a rutted path. "About a hundred yards to our left is one of the prettiest stargazing spots in the world."

He followed the trail to the top of a low hill and turned off the ignition. He couldn't read Poppy's expression in the dim light, but noticed she gripped the door handle with white-knuckled intensity.

"Come on, sweetheart." Gently pulling the passenger door open, Josh extended his hand in invitation. "I promise we won't stay long."

She gave him a tentative smile and wordlessly placed her hand in his. The gesture held such trust, Josh felt his heart swell with tenderness.

A million stars glittered in the night sky. They stood for a moment in the stillness, heads tilted upward in awe.

"I don't think I've ever seen them look more beautiful." She shivered slightly and wrapped the cotton shawl more tightly around her. "I guess I didn't come prepared for stargazing."

"I did." Josh rummaged in the rear of the jeep and came back with a soft down quilt. Gently, he placed his hands around her waist and lifted her onto the warm hood of the jeep, arranging the quilt around her shoulders. She couldn't have weighed more than a hundred pounds. But oh, how enticingly those pounds had been distributed.

"Let me keep you warm," he whispered. "Just for a few minutes." He slid between her knees and pressed her slender body to his. Her hands came up to stroke his head where it rested on her breast. He could feel her heart pound, her breathing quicken.

Her response provoked a heated one of his own.

Unable to stop himself, he drew her closer, raining warm, tender kisses down her bare throat to the lacy top of her peasant blouse.

"Poppy, darling," he murmured. "I want you so much. More than I've ever wanted anyone."

Josh's words registered slowly through the haze of desire his touch created. *More than I've ever wanted anyone.* How many times has he said that before? Poppy wondered. And how many more times would he say those words after he left her and Providence far behind?

Her eyes flew open. "No!" In a desperate attempt to regain control of her emotions, she shoved Josh away. She watched in astonishment as he stumbled backward, lost his footing, and landed on his rear in the dirt.

He sat sprawled on the desert floor, blinking up at her like the young barn own she'd surprised in the lava tube. For a moment she had an insane impulse to giggle, but quickly squelched it. His ego—and his rear end—had been bruised enough already.

"Gosh, I didn't mean to push you that hard." She scrambled down from the jeep's hood. Uncertain what to do or say, she blurted out the truth. "I'm sorry. I just can't be another girl you leave behind."

Josh picked himself up and gingerly dusted off his doubly abused backside. Served him right, he thought. If he couldn't keep his hands off Poppy for fifteen minutes, how would he ever convince her of his honorable intentions? Or convince himself, for that matter.

"I deserved that." He lifted Poppy's chin and kissed her lightly on the nose. "Come on, sunshine. We need to talk."

"What about?" Poppy asked.

"About our future."

When they were settled snugly in the jeep, with the engine humming and the heater on low, Josh took a deep breath and began.

"I've given this a lot of thought. I care about you, Poppy. More than I've ever cared for anyone. I think you have feelings for me, too." He paused, hoping for an affirmative answer.

Poppy nodded. Her big blue eyes regarded him with both hope and wariness.

"When I was in Los Angeles last week I met with the company that's financing my documentary. They told me I'll have to cut my production schedule. That means I'll be leaving sooner than I'd planned."

Pain flashed across Poppy's expressive features. Unwilling to hurt her for even a moment, Josh hurried on. "I want you to come with me, Poppy. I'd like to hire you to work for Outback Productions. With your knowledge and love of the outdoors, you'll be a natural. You can help me scout locations. I'll teach you to use the camera, if you like. There are a million things you could do to earn your pay."

"And one of those things wouldn't be sleeping with the boss, would it?"

Josh felt as though he'd been slapped. How could he

not have anticipated her reaction? "Absolutely not. There are no strings attached."

"Let me see if I have this straight. You tell me you care about me and then you ask me to come with you with 'no strings attached?' "

Josh pounded the steering wheel in frustration. "I knew I wouldn't get it right. What I'm trying to say is, I can't bear the thought of losing you. I want you to share my life, as a friend, a lover, a co-worker, whatever you feel comfortable with. I promise not to touch you unless you're sure it's right. It won't be easy, but at least I'll have your company."

Poppy sat quietly, thinking about Josh's offer. She wasn't cold anymore, at least, not on the outside. The cold, dark stillness of the night seemed to have filtered into her soul. She knew from the depths of her being what her answer had to be.

"When you asked me if I cared for you, I didn't tell the truth. Or at least, not all of it. The truth is, I've loved you from the first moment I saw you. I didn't know it at the time. I thought you were the most exasperating, arrogant, egotistical man I'd ever met. When I got to know you, I discovered how wrong I was, about almost everything."

"Then come with me, Poppy. We'll watch the sunrise over the Sahara Desert, swim in the turquoise waters off Anguilla."

She shook her head sadly. "It sounds wonderful. But I can't."

"Why not?"

"You said it yourself, the night we met. You're a rolling stone. I could travel with you for a while, maybe even a year or two. Eventually, I'd come back to Providence and you'd go on to the next exotic place. I couldn't bear that, Josh. I don't want us to end in bitterness and regret."

Josh took Poppy's hand in both of his. He lifted it to his lips and kissed her slender fingers. "It wasn't much of an offer, was it?"

She laughed shakily. Outside, the pinpoints of light blurred into an unearthly glow. "It was a lovely offer. I just don't think it would work."

"For what it's worth, I've never extended that invitation to anyone else."

"I know." A single tear trickled down her cheek, soon followed by another.

"I hate the thought of leaving you."

Poppy swiped a hand across her eyes and turned to Josh with a determined smile. "Let's not think about it, then, or talk about it. Let's just enjoy the time we have left."

"Easier said than done, I think. For you, my darling, I'll try."

They held hands on the way home. Poppy felt strangely peaceful, gazing through half-closed eyes at the dim shapes of creosote bushes and cacti that rushed past her window.

Josh wanted her, cared for her, had asked her to share his life. *But he didn't say he loves me.* She pushed the unwelcome thought away. She knew the pain of separation lay ahead. All the more reason to cherish these few moments together.

She awakened from a light, dream-filled sleep as the jeep came to a stop in front of Poppy's Place. "Slim," she said.

"What's that, sunshine? Still dreaming?"

She sat up and brushed the curls off her forehead. "When I woke up just now, it came to me. The name for your jeep."

"Slim." He rolled the word over his tongue. "Like the heroine in 'To Have and Have Not.' It's perfect."

Maybe you'll think of me when you drive her, Poppy thought. And then aloud, "Will you be staying over this weekend?"

Josh didn't answer right away. He stepped out of the jeep and quickly strode around to open her door. "I'm afraid not," he said. "I have to be in Los Angeles tomorrow afternoon for another session with Mother Nature's Workshop. I'll be back this way late Sunday night. If it's okay with you and Aunt El, I'd like to park the motor homes beside the cafe and make this our base of operations for the next couple of weeks."

The blast of cool air had a less chilling effect than Josh's words. *A couple of weeks.* Was that all they had left? Trying desperately to cling to her resolve, Poppy said, "Of course, but why the change of plan?"

Josh put his arm around her shoulders as they walked

toward the cafe. "We'll have to pick up the pace for the remainder of our time here. Even with longer days and less break time, we won't be able to shoot everything I'd planned. If you're willing to put together breakfast and pack us a lunch, I think we can cover quite a lot of territory."

The tears she'd struggled to keep in check all evening flowed freely now. Josh sat on the porch steps and drew her into his lap. When the storm subsided, he handed her a clean bandana to wipe her face.

She hiccupped. "Dang!" She wiped her streaming eyes then blew her nose. Another hiccup.

"I bet Lauren Bacall wouldn't do that." She took a deep breath, closed her eyes, and counted to sixty. Finally she exhaled and looked at him.

"Feeling better?" he asked.

She was grateful he hadn't laughed. "I'm sorry. I guess it didn't seem real before. Now you've put a number on it. Two weeks. Only fourteen more days and you'll be gone."

Josh pulled her against his hard chest and nuzzled her hair. "I didn't say exactly fourteen days. It could be a little longer. We still have some time to think things over."

Poppy sniffled and looked up at him. "Two weeks in the springtime can bring lots of changes, can't they?"

He kissed her forehead before she snuggled back into his embrace. "They sure can."

Josh's words comforted her, as did the solid feeling

of his arms around her. He hadn't run away this time, she realized. Not when she rejected his offer or cried. Not even when she shoved him down in the dirt. Through it all, he'd stayed with her. She wasn't sure what Josh had in mind, but she wouldn't give up hope. She just had to be patient and give the magic between them a chance to work.

She turned to him with glistening eyes. "I'm sure Aunt El will be happy to have you park in our lot. To tell you the truth, I've been feeling guilty about leaving the cafe every day. This is our busiest season, and even with extra help I know she's working too hard."

"Thank you." Josh's gratitude was reflected in the warmth of his gaze. "I'd better get started. Slim and I have miles to go before we sleep."

"Promise you'll stop if you get tired."

Josh pressed her hand to his lips, then repeated solemnly, "I promise to stop when I'm tired. I promise to dream of you when I close my eyes. And I promise to count the minutes until I see you again. Goodnight, my sunshine."

Chapter Nine

T rue to his word, Josh arrived at Poppy's Place early Sunday evening. Somehow he'd made it through his meeting with Mother Nature's Workshop and the rest of the weekend, mechanically going about his business while his thoughts and his heart remained in Providence.

As he got out of the car after the long drive from Los Angeles, the anticipation of seeing her had his pulse racing. He bent to tug his jeans over his boots, and when he straightened she stood in the doorway as if summoned by the force of his longing.

She looked so adorable there, barefoot, in shorts and a lacy little top. She paused for only a moment before flying down the porch steps and into his arms.

Desperate for the scent and feel of her, Josh planted

a succession of quick kisses on her cheeks and fore-head before coming to rest on her sweet lips. He wasn't sure how long the kiss lasted. It could have been an eternity or maybe only a moment. When he could bear no more, he crushed her to him. "My sweet Poppy. How I've missed you."

A feminine chuckle bubbled to the surface from somewhere deep within her. It held the confident note of a woman who instinctively knows her power over a man. Perhaps she had bewitched him in the beginning, Josh reflected. But at some point he'd become a willing captive. He no longer had any desire to resist; her enchantment was the sweetest he'd ever known.

"Come on," she said, taking his hand. "Aunt El has your dinner warming in the oven."

Sitting by the big potbellied stove in the corner of the cafe, Josh watched the twilight deepen on the Providence Range. For once, he barely tasted Aunt El's delicious food. He consumed it one-handedly, unwilling to relinquish his hold on Poppy.

Although the stove's warmth felt good tonight, in a couple of weeks it wouldn't be needed. The lush green tendrils of spring were spreading throughout the East Mojave. And with the spring, he'd be gone.

"You look tired," Poppy said.

Josh pushed back his plate. "That's what Elaine told me. Only she didn't put it quite so kindly."

"You saw Elaine and the girls? How are they?"

"They're doing great. The girls are growing like

weeds. I have to say, though, Elaine isn't too impressed with me. I talked to her about our discussion Friday night. I hope you don't mind."

"Everybody needs a sympathetic ear now and then. What did she say?"

Josh smiled wryly. Sympathetic didn't exactly describe Elaine's reaction to his tale. "She said you sound like a wonderful person and I'd be a fool to let you go. She also said I deserved to be shoved in the dirt and if any of the other women I've dated had had half a brain, it would have happened long ago and many more times."

"You told her I *shoved* you?" Poppy gasped, mortification coloring her cheeks.

Josh nodded. "And furthermore, she said if a man made such a lame, insulting proposal to her, she'd have kicked his butt all the way to Bakersfield. My big sister thinks it's high time I grew up."

Poppy continued to look at him with those big innocent blue eyes.

Josh shifted uncomfortably and then took the plunge. "I've done a lot of thinking this weekend. There's something I have to ask you. Please don't be offended, but I need to know. Have you ever been in a serious relationship?"

Poppy remained silent for a moment, considering the man and the question. For once the teasing gleam in his eye was gone. He looked serious, maybe even a little afraid of her reaction. His expression touched her. "No more than you, my love," she said softly.

"I don't understand."

She spoke slowly, choosing her words with care. "A couple of years ago, right after Uncle Mike died, Aunt El and I closed up the business and spent a whole summer in San Diego. I met a young man there, a surfer. He was very sweet. I thought I was in love, but when he wanted to be intimate, I couldn't. Maybe because of my mother and the mistakes she made. Maybe I felt too vulnerable, so soon after Uncle Mike's death. I'm not really sure why. Somehow, I just knew it wasn't right."

"How about the men around here? Wasn't there ever anyone special?"

Poppy snorted. "It's hard to feel romantic about someone who used to throw spit wads at you. I've known most of these guys since fourth grade. They're like my brothers."

"I have a feeling I'm not going to like the answer, but I'll ask anyway. Why did you say no more than me?"

"Because although you've had physical relationships, you've never given your heart to anyone. In that way we're alike."

Poppy got up and took Josh's plate to the kitchen. She returned with two glasses of cold lemonade. "And now there's something I want to ask you."

Josh picked up his lemonade and took a long drink, eyeing her over the rim. "Shoot." He set the glass down with a clunk.

"Tell me about your mom and dad's divorce."

"Ah, she aims right at the heart of my emotional immaturity. I think I told you a little bit that day in Wildhorse Canyon. Mom wanted a career. Her life was changing and Dad couldn't accept it. He started going out with the boys after work. He was staying out later and later, hitting the bottle pretty hard.

"Mom finally got fed up with the late hours, the drinking, and the total lack of support. One night, after an especially loud and ugly argument, she asked him to leave."

"You still saw him, didn't you?"

"Not for a while. Dad was so bitter and self-destructive, in the beginning he shut us all out."

Remembered pain roughened Josh's voice as he continued. "My dad had always been my best buddy. He took me hiking and fishing, carried me home piggyback when I was too tired to walk. Then one day he just disappeared. Mom did her best to fill in, but with a demanding job, two kids to support, and a house to take care of, not to mention the trauma of the divorce, she really had a full plate."

"It must have been a terrible time for you." Sympathetic tears filled Poppy's eyes.

"It was. After about a year, things started to turn around. Dad got involved in a twelve-step program and made his amends to all of us. It took me a while, but I forgave him. I think because we'd been so close, his rejection hit me especially hard. Elaine was hurt by the divorce and Dad checking out on us, too, but she was three years older. She had her friends and activities and a great role model in Mom. She handled the whole thing a lot better than I did. Or at least, I thought so at the time."

"What happened to change your mind?" Poppy asked.

"It's funny, isn't it, how history repeats itself? Elaine married young. Her husband, Don, seemed all right at first. They had a couple of beautiful little girls together. When Elaine was pregnant with my youngest niece, Don left her for another woman. It turned out he'd been playing around the whole time. Elaine was so desperate to keep her family together, she ignored his infidelities. She kept everything to herself, pretending they were a happy family. Mom and I had no idea anything was wrong until the day Don walked out."

"How terrible. Elaine must have been devastated."

Josh nodded. "She was, but with the help of a good therapist she's become stronger and more loving than ever. I just hope someday she'll meet a man who's worthy of her."

"An experience like that could sure make a person shy away from commitment."

"Elaine is very selective about her male friends," Josh said. "As she should be, for her sake and the girls'."

Poppy spoke softly. "I wasn't talking about Elaine."

He wrested an imaginary arrow from his chest. "Another bull's-eye. You're right. Elaine's divorce added to my feeling that relationships don't last and commitment only leads to pain."

Poppy crossed to where Josh sprawled sideways in his chair, one hand gripping his lemonade, a long leg extending toward the center of the cafe. She snuggled into his lap and wrapped her arms around his neck. "And so, Mr. Josh O'Donnell, it seems a couple of old singletons whose lives are continents apart have finally found one another. What are we going to do about it?"

Josh buried his face in Poppy's soft, springy hair. He felt more at home here, with her in his arms, than he'd ever felt in his life. "I wish I knew, sweetheart. I wish I knew."

"Did you have a nice time last night?" Aunt El asked.

They sat at the table closest to the cash register, enjoying a break in business and a mid-morning cup of tea. Poppy had been up early, putting together a quick breakfast for the crew. She looked into the kind blue eyes of the woman sitting opposite her and recognized an invitation for shared confidences.

"Josh told me about his parents' divorce and the breakup of his sister's marriage. Elaine's husband abandoned her and the three little girls."

Aunt El's eyes flashed over the rim of her cup. "'Tis hard to imagine a person with a heart so hard. He'll regret it one day."

"I sincerely hope so," Poppy said. "I think I understand Josh a little better now. His family's problems have made him afraid of commitment."

"Oh? It sounds like he's thinking about commitment now. And if he has half as much sense as I think he does, he'll be making his mind up soon."

Poppy felt her face warming. Should she tell Aunt El she was in love with Josh? If she spoke the words, she feared their magic would disappear like crystal dewdrops on a spiderweb in the first rays of the sun. She wasn't ready yet to share the secrets of her heart, even with Aunt El.

"How's that new friend of yours?" she asked. "He was looking mighty handsome at the Rattlesnake Ball."

Aunt El accepted the change of subject without comment. Although always ready to listen, El had an unerring instinct about when to let Poppy sort things out for herself.

"He did look nice, didn't he? Homer is a fine man, and a talented one. He's thinking of starting a newspaper in Providence."

Poppy set down her cup. "A newspaper? I thought Homer wrote poetry."

"It'll be a mix of literature and local news, with desert stories, cowboy poetry, photos, perhaps some artwork or drawings, and some of Homer's work. He'll invite everyone in the East Mojave to contribute. If you know any schoolchildren who have original poems or stories about our area, he'd like to include them too."

"That's a wonderful idea!" Poppy said. "It's just

what Providence needs. Ashley Evans loves to write and draw. I know she'll have something."

Aunt El beamed. "I thought we'd keep a stack of Homer's newspapers right by the cash register. Visitors to the national preserve will be able to take a little bit of Providence home with them."

Poppy picked up their empty cups. "That quiet friend of yours is turning into quite an asset to our community."

Aunt El looked as pleased as if Poppy had just presented her with a check for a million dollars. "Still waters run deep," she said.

The days took on a bittersweet rhythm and a poignant sweetness. The crew left before dawn each morning and often didn't return to the cafe until well past the dinner hour. After Meg and Carlos had eaten and retired to their motor homes, and Aunt El had made herself scarce on some pretext or another, Josh lingered in the cafe. He and Poppy talked about the events of their days.

The crew was working its way across Devil's Playground through the Mojave River Sink to Afton Canyon. Josh wanted to record a sampling of the plant and animal life in the far western reaches of the national preserve. He told Poppy what they'd filmed each day, and they discussed how the segments should be used in his documentary.

Poppy shared her plans for enlarging the hiking section of the store. She told Josh what was sprouting in her garden, which of the children had stopped by after school, or relayed news about one of the locals who had become a mutual friend.

Although he caught only a few hours' sleep each night, Josh awoke feeling invigorated and refreshed. He seemed to draw energy from the hours he spent with Poppy. Meg and Carlos teased him about living on love, but Josh didn't mind. His resolve grew stronger with each passing day. A plan was taking shape in his mind. It would soon be time to put it into action.

Poppy woke early on a Friday morning to the sounds of spring. Mama and papa robin and their hungry brood were making quite a racket in the mulberry tree outside her window. Through the parted curtains she saw moisture glistening on the newly leafed grapevines, washed clean by the night's gentle rain. Although some gray clouds lingered, the weather report said they'd soon be moving across the East Mojave Desert and on to Arizona. *Just as Josh would soon be drifting on, to another exotic locale, another adventure, perhaps even another love.*

Throwing off the covers, Poppy sat up and rubbed the sleep out of her eyes. Enough of that, she told herself firmly. She had promised to enjoy every day she and Josh had left. She wasn't about to waste this gorgeous morning lying in bed feeling sorry for herself.

Still, as she brushed her teeth and pulled her hair into

a tight French braid, Poppy felt the small hard knot in her stomach return. It had been there every day since she'd learned Josh was leaving. And now there were so few days left.

She was surprised to see Josh and Aunt El sitting alone in the dining room, heads together, talking in low tones. How long had it been since she'd seen them sit in just that way, planning to convince her to accept Josh's offer of a catering job? Watching them from the doorway, she had the uneasy feeling that once again, the two of them shared a secret.

"Hey, I thought you were spending the night in Afton Canyon."

Both heads popped up. "Good morning, sunshine. Sleep well?" Josh asked.

The sparkle in his eye confirmed her suspicion. "Okay, you two, what kind of plot are you hatching now?" She helped herself to a cup of coffee from the stainless steel pot on their table.

"A plot, she says." Aunt El's blue eyes grew wide with injured innocence. "Since when is a picnic in Ivanpah Valley a plot?"

"Ivanpah Valley!" It was one of Poppy's favorite springtime destinations. With all the rain they'd had this winter, the wildflowers in the valley would be glorious. "But what about your production schedule?" she asked, turning to Josh.

"Carlos is perfectly capable of filming Afton Canyon without me. In fact, it will do him good to be in charge.

He's been ready to work independently for a long time."

"And I have Sue Mason coming to help out at the cafe," Aunt El put in.

"I guess it's settled then." Poppy's eyes met Josh's over the rim of her cup. Despite her intuition that something was afoot, the prospect of a whole day with Josh filled her with joyous anticipation.

"You'd best be on your way," Aunt El said. "Sue will be here any minute. Poppy, take a couple of those fresh cinnamon rolls. I'll not have you going off without breakfast. Have a lovely time, darlin'." She kissed Poppy on the cheek, then hurried toward the kitchen, wiping her eyes with a corner of her apron.

The valley was more beautiful than Poppy had ever seen it. She and Josh hiked hand in hand over a landscape magically come to life. The normally brown terrain was covered with delicate green. Patches of lavender and yellow, luminous white and lipstick red vied for their attention. Poppy pointed out desert asters, dandelions, lilies, monkey flowers, and sand verbena. Even the squat barrel cactus got into the act, bristling with vivid fuschia blossoms.

They stopped at the base of a low, boulder-strewn hill. Tall grasses sprang up between the rocks. A few bright orange desert poppies had found a tenuous foothold in the sparse soil. Josh watched from below as Poppy scrambled over boulders.

"Come on." She motioned for him to join her. "The view is incredible up here."

"It's pretty incredible from where I stand, too." Shifting the picnic basket to his left hand, he began to climb.

Josh was unusually quiet during lunch, but Poppy didn't mind. The sun warmed her face as they shared a boulder and the contents of the picnic basket. Occasionally, she reached over to smooth his silky hair or rest a hand on his knee. She was rewarded with a smile or an answering caress.

These last two weeks had been the most wonderful of her life. Although their physical intimacy had been limited to hand-holding and a goodnight kiss, Josh's touch, full of love and tenderness, brought tears to her eyes. She understood his restraint and it made her feel even more special. He cared for her enough to wait until the time was right for both of them.

A movement in the wash below caught her attention. Sitting suddenly upright, she watched what appeared to be a medium-sized brown rock lumber slowly toward a patch of wildflowers. "Look!" she whispered. At that moment a wizened head stretched out to take a bite from the blossoms.

"I'll be darned. A desert tortoise. It's the first time I've seen one in the wild. And me without my camera," Josh said.

"I was hoping we'd spot one. The wildflowers are like candy to tortoises. It's a little late in the day for this guy to be out. They usually feed in the morning and evening and hide in their burrows at midday," Poppy said.

"I guess he's enjoying the fine spring weather, too."

"We could come back next week," she suggested. "This is prime tortoise habitat. With a little luck, we might find another."

"I won't be here next week, Poppy."

The statement hit her like a fist in the stomach. "I see." Her voice sounded stiff and hurt, she knew, but it was the best she could manage.

"Mother Nature's Workshop wants me back in L.A. to start post-production work. When I finish, I have an assignment in Belize. I was hoping you'd come with me."

"We've already discussed that. We both know it wouldn't work."

Josh shook his head. "I'm upping the ante."

To her astonishment, he dropped to one knee on the rocky ground and took her hand in his. "I love you, Penelope Sullivan. Will you marry me?"

Poppy's heart soared. Josh loved her. He'd asked her to be his wife. How often had she dreamt of this moment? To have a husband, a home, and family. Her first impulse was to shout "Yes!" but a cold whisper of caution made her pause. *What exactly was Josh offering? Could he possibly want the kind of life she needed and longed for?*

"Are you ready to settle down, then?" she asked.

"I can't right away. I have commitments. In another

year or two, I plan to cut back on my traveling. Then we can settle down in Providence and start a family. Come with me, Poppy. I love you and I know you love me. That's the important part. Everything else can be worked out."

Poppy felt as if she were outside her body. She saw herself sitting on the sun-warmed boulder, surrounded by the delicate beauty of spring with the man she loved kneeling before her. She knew this was a turning point in her life. When she gave her answer, everything would change. She wanted desperately to stay in this moment just a little longer, to delay taking the plunge into the unknown. But Josh was waiting for an answer.

"When I first came to Providence, Aunt El and Uncle Mike promised me I'd always have a home here. It took some time, but finally I believed them. I made myself a promise, too. I promised I would never leave the East Mojave. This land is a part of me, Josh. If I said yes, and traveled the world with you, it wouldn't be Poppy Sullivan you'd have along, but only a ghost of the woman you think you love."

The look of hurt on Josh's face filled her with remorse.

"You still doubt that I'm capable of loving you," he said.

"No, Josh, I don't. I just think that love means different things to different people. To me, love means commitment, stability, a home, and family. I know you intend to settle down someday. I believe you want children. But would a year or two turn into three or four or ten? I don't know the answer to that question. I don't think you do either."

Poppy struggled for a way to make him understand. "Look at the tortoise down there. Even with the perils of desert life, he's thriving. But if you took him away from his home range, he'd die of exposure or starvation. I'm like that tortoise. If I left the East Mojave, a part of me would die, too."

Josh slowly got up and began packing the picnic basket. "The tortoise is a solitary creature, isn't it?"

"Yes."

"That's what you'll be, Poppy. Unless you can open your heart enough to trust someone. Sometimes love requires a leap of faith."

Those were the last words he spoke until they reached Providence.

Chapter Ten

The rest of the afternoon passed in a blur. Poppy trailed miserably behind Josh to the truck and endured a silent ride back to Providence. Her heart felt as if it would shatter with every rut in the dusty desert road.

She tried once again to talk to him when they stopped in front of the cafe, but Josh was cold and unresponsive. He gripped the steering wheel, staring straight ahead while she fumbled for the right words, words that could soothe his hurt and salvage their love.

Josh cut her off. "I'll send you a check for your catering services. That is, if you think you can trust me."

Poppy recoiled as though he'd slapped her. *Please don't go!* she wanted to cry. *Not like this. I don't want it to end this way.* Pride made her swallow the words. What would they accomplish? She'd made her decision and Josh obviously wanted to get away from her and Providence as soon as possible.

Poppy forced herself to open the door. "Goodbye, Josh," she whispered, then turned and ran blindly across the parking lot. Oblivious to the startled looks of late afternoon customers, she dashed headlong through the store and cafe. Finally, safe in her bedroom, she let the tears flow.

Sometime later, she was awakened by a light tapping. Feeling groggy and disoriented, she lifted her head from the damp pillow. It was dark outside. She must have slept through the late afternoon and into the evening.

Then she remembered. She curled into the fetal position as the pain gripped her. *Josh is gone.* She had turned him down, rejected his proposal of marriage, and he'd walked out of her life forever.

"Poppy, darlin'. Are you awake?" Aunt El's head appeared in the doorway. "I brought you some soup."

Poppy sat up and fumbled with the lamp on her nightstand. "Come in."

Aunt El shoved aside the clutter on a round table in front of Poppy's garden window to make room for her supper tray. She sat on the edge of the bed. "It might help to talk about it."

Aunt El's sympathetic tone and warm, familiar presence threatened to start the tears afresh. Poppy took a deep breath, willing herself to be calm. "You knew, didn't you?"

"That Josh was going to propose? Yes, I did. He

asked my permission to take you away for a while. He said he wanted to be sure I could manage this place by myself. And he promised you'd both be coming back here one day, to settle down and raise a family. He did ask you, didn't he?"

Poppy nodded miserably. "I said no."

"But why, darlin'? Any fool can see that you're head over heels in love with him."

"I couldn't leave Providence, Aunt El. This is my home, the only place I've ever felt like I belonged. I'm sure Josh means well. But how can a man who's spent practically his whole life on the road be happy in one place?"

Aunt El patted her hand. "I can't give you the answers you're looking for, Poppy. You have to find them for yourself. I will say I believe Josh O'Donnell is a fine young man and an honorable one. When in doubt, dear, listen to your heart."

Poppy held tight to a bedraggled stuffed bunny, a relic of her childhood. "Why couldn't I have fallen in love with someone who wants the same things I do? I've always dreamed of a marriage like you and Uncle Mike had. You shared a life you both loved. Is that too much to ask?"

Aunt El turned her face to the windows. Her gaze seemed focused on a distant time and place. For a moment, Poppy wondered if El had heard her.

"Aunt El?"

The older woman drew her attention back to the

present. She smiled and patted Poppy's hand. "Yes, darlin'. I'm here. I was just thinking about the first couple of years we spent in the East Mojave, before you came to live with us."

"Tell me about them."

El picked up the bunny and absently smoothed its ears as she spoke. "It was always Mike's dream to live in the desert. He loved the clean air and the wide open spaces. When he took an early retirement, we bought the store and moved to Providence. But you see, it was Mike's dream, not mine.

"At first, I thought I'd die from loneliness. Whole days went by without a single person stopping at the store. We were barely scraping by on Mike's pension, trying to get the business established. I wanted to move back to the city, but Mike refused. He had a stubborn streak, my Mike did."

"Did you think about leaving Providence alone?" Even now, the thought of Aunt El and Uncle Mike splitting up shook her to the core.

"I threatened to go a time or two. Then I realized I loved that hard-headed Irishman too much to ask him to give up his dream. I made up my mind to stay and make a good life here. From that day on, things began to get better. Business picked up, Mike and I were happier, but something was still missing. The day we brought you to Providence, it became my home, too."

"You miss Uncle Mike a lot, don't you?"

For just a moment, Aunt El looked sadder than

Poppy had seen her since the days immediately following Mike's funeral. "Aye. I think of him every day. We had our differences but I never doubted his love for me, nor mine for him. We lived together thirty-five years and I wouldn't change a minute of it."

Long after Aunt El departed, Poppy lay awake. Had she done the right thing? Or was she giving up her chance at happiness out of fear? Josh's words kept running through her brain. *"The tortoise is a solitary creature, isn't it? That's what you'll be unless you can open your heart enough to trust someone."*

It's not fair, she thought, pounding her pillow. Why should she have to choose between the life she'd always wanted and the man she loved?

Josh asked you to marry him, promised to settle down and raise a family in Providence. You wouldn't even meet him halfway, a small voice within her accused.

I made a promise, too, Poppy argued. *I promised I'd never leave the East Mojave. Mama spent most of her life looking for love and security. I've found it, right here in Providence. I won't give that up.*

Then why are you so miserable? the voice asked.

As she lay awake, staring into the darkness, a coyote raised its mournful cry to the moon. She hadn't felt so alone since she was a child in the foster home.

Poppy took advantage of a temporary lull in business to catch her breath and go through the day's receipts. The lunch rush was just winding down.

She'd been running between the cafe and store all morning.

Not bad, she thought. Not bad at all. If they continued to do this well, she could afford to keep Sue Mason on after the tourist season. Aunt El had been training Sue to do some of the backup work in the kitchen, and the rancher's wife had proven herself a quick and efficient helper.

In addition to the flood of spring visitors, many retirees and even a few new families with children had decided to make the East Mojave their home. It was the busiest season Poppy could remember.

Maybe it was time for her to think about going back to school to get her teaching degree. She closed the cash drawer with a sigh. Who was she kidding? Nothing sparked her interest or enthusiasm anymore. Things that were once so important to her, the little everyday triumphs, her hopes and her dreams, seemed dull and colorless without Josh to share them.

He'd been gone for a little over two weeks and she missed him terribly. Not just physically, although that was a powerful ache in itself. She missed his companionship, the comfort of his presence at the end of the day. She missed his laugh and the teasing gleam in his eye. She even missed his habit of sneaking up on her. Life was never dull with Josh in the vicinity.

Was she ready to take that leap of faith? Could she give up everything she held dear to link her life with Josh's?

"A penny for your thoughts."

The familiar turn of phrase jarred Poppy out of her reverie. They were the words Josh had spoken the first time he'd invaded her garden. And again when Aunt El invited him to dinner. Only this time, the voice was unmistakably feminine.

"Meg! What a wonderful surprise!" She hurried around the counter and gave the vivacious redhead a hug.

Meg set down the wicker hamper she'd been carrying to return Poppy's embrace. "How you doing, girl?" she asked, drawing back to peer at her friend's face.

Poppy was embarrassed by the tears that sprang to her eyes under Meg's sympathetic scrutiny. "As well as can be expected, I guess. I've been meaning to call you but we've been so busy here." Her glance lighted on the picnic basket. "Did Josh ask you to return that?"

Meg nodded.

The tears spilled over Poppy's eyelids and rolled down her cheeks. "Oh Meg, I wanted to call. But I knew I couldn't talk without crying. I can't seem to turn off the faucet lately."

Meg put her arm around Poppy and squeezed her shoulder reassuringly. "Come on. I have something to show you that I think will make you feel better."

"Cover for me, will you, Sue?" Poppy called.

She led Meg to a table in the far corner of the dining room where they could talk in private. She'd already treated the cafe's customers to enough drama to keep the locals talking for weeks. Every rancher, rockhound, and retiree for miles around would have heard about her mad dash through the cafe, and she was sure the story had lost nothing in the telling.

Without prelude, Meg handed her an envelope. Poppy instantly recognized the firm, slanting handwriting. She'd seen notebooks filled with it at Outback Production's campsites in the East Mojave. Josh was meticulous about documenting his findings on both paper and film.

She paused for only a moment to gaze wonderingly at Meg, her heart pounding. Was it possible Josh had forgiven her, that he understood why she couldn't come with him? Or maybe, maybe he loved her enough to stay? Josh's final remark seared her brain. *I'll send you a check for your catering services. That is, if you think you can trust me.*

"Go ahead," Meg said. "It has your name on it."

That's all it is, Poppy told herself. *Just a check*. Still, she couldn't control the trembling of her fingers as she tore open the envelope.

A single sheet of white paper was folded inside. Poppy barely noticed the check that fluttered to the ground as she opened the note and began to read.

Poppy,
By the time you receive this I'll be on my way to Belize to do the advance work for my next documentary. I couldn't leave without apologizing for my knavish behavior last week. I was hurt and dis-

appointed. Who wouldn't be, after being turned down by the fairest maid in all the land? I hope you'll find it in your heart to forgive me. I'll always love you.

Josh

P.S. If you change your mind, just whistle.

Poppy read the note through twice. *Josh still loves me.* Suddenly, she knew with absolute certainty what she had to do. Her heart pounded out a message, loud and clear. This time she was ready to listen.

"What time does his plane leave?" she asked, jumping up from the table.

"Aeromexico, Flight Two-eight-nine, departs Los Angeles at 7 P.M. You can still make it if you leave right away," Meg answered.

Poppy was out of her apron and halfway to the door when she whirled around suddenly. "What about the store and cafe?" she asked.

"I can stay and help out. I had some waitress experience in my younger days. I'll just call Pete and tell him not to expect me until tomorrow morning."

Poppy gazed at her friend with affection. "You didn't come all the way to Providence to deliver a note and a picnic basket, did you?"

"I have to confess, I had hopes," Meg admitted. "Now get out of here. I'll explain to Aunt El."

Poppy made a quick stop in her room to grab her purse and a sweater. Holding the bush hat Josh had given her firmly on her head, she sprinted through the garden gate to the parking lot. As she turned the key in the ignition, one thought filled her brain. She *had* to make it to the airport on time.

"Rover, don't fail me now!"

It was dark by the time she turned into the short-term parking garage at the Los Angeles International Airport. She yanked her ticket out of the automated parking attendant and gripped the steering wheel as she waited impatiently for the stanchion to lift.

Six-thirty. Only thirty minutes until Josh's plane lifted off. Well, she hadn't made it this far for nothing. Come hell or high water, she was going to catch that man before he got on the plane.

She circled around and around in the parking structure, searching for an empty space. It seemed all the inhabitants of this sprawling metropolis who hadn't crowded onto the freeways this evening were flying out of LAX. Finally, on the uppermost level, she found a place to park. Within seconds, she vaulted out of the car, barely noticing the stiffness of her limbs as she raced for the elevator.

Six-forty. The ride down to the ticketing and departure area seemed interminable. Finally, the elevator door opened to reveal a terminal swarming with people. Businessmen in tailored suits strode briskly toward the departure gates. Mothers hurried along, clutching the hands of wide-eyed children. Lovers, young and old, walked arm in arm through the crowd, aware only of each other. All of this registered vaguely as Poppy took a deep breath and plunged into the flow of humanity.

Ah! There it was. A knot of onlookers gathered around a monitor showing arrivals and departures. She craned her neck to see over the heads of people in front of her. What she wouldn't give for a couple of extra inches! Finally she spotted it. Aeromexico, Flight Two-eight-nine, departing for Belize, on time, gate A3.

Dang! Why couldn't the flight have been delayed? She turned and jogged in the direction of the A gates, tossing "excuse me's" to folks she bumped and jostled along the way.

By the time she reached the security checkpoint, her heart was pumping as if she'd drunk a dozen cups of coffee. The bush hat hung down her back and her hair flew in every direction.

Six-fifty. Only ten minutes!

"Pardon me," she said breathlessly to the attendant at the gate. "I have to talk to someone on Flight Two-eight-nine."

The woman eyed her cooly. "Do you have a ticket?" she asked.

"No, but . . ."

"I'm sorry. I can't allow anyone past this point without a ticket."

For one insane moment, Poppy considered rushing past her.

Oh sure, and then they'll drag you off in handcuffs.

She'd forgotten about the tougher security measures at all the nation's airports. The long drive from Providence, her wild dash through the airport, had been doomed from the start. There was no way she could reach Josh in time. Her shoulders sagged as she started to walk away.

"Excuse me, miss. What is the problem?"

A tall, slender brunette in an Aeromexico uniform regarded her sympathetically. To Poppy, she looked like an angel.

"I need to get a message to one of the passengers on Flight 289 to Belize. It leaves in ten minutes"

The woman chuckled. "I do not think it will leave without me. Give me your message quickly."

Poppy pulled a notepad from her purse and hurriedly scrawled:

I'm ready to make the leap. Will you catch me?
Poppy

She folded the note over once and handed it to the flight attendant. "Please give this to Josh O'Donnell. And thank you. You'll never know how much this means to me."

The woman gave her an enigmatic smile. Then she turned and hurried through the security checkpoint.

A voice on the public address system announced "Boarding is completed for Aeromexico Flight Two-eight-nine, to Mexico City and Belize City. All ticketed passengers should be on the plane."

Poppy sank into a chair where she could see passengers entering and leaving the checkpoint. All the adrenaline flowed out of her, leaving a curious emptiness. She felt like one of the gourds she'd collected as a child: hard, dry, and brittle on the outside, hollow on the inside. She was too late. Even if the flight attendant delivered her message, what right did she have to expect Josh to get off the plane and come running into her arms?

None. None at all, she told herself. Josh was on a business trip. All his arrangements and reservations had been made. In just a few minutes, Flight 289 would take off and he'd be on his way to Belize.

Still, if he really loves me, maybe he'll stay.

The minutes ticked away. *Seven o'clock, seven-ten, seven-thirty.* She knew it was time to go home. She hadn't been able to talk to Josh, but at least she'd written him the note. That was worth something, wasn't it?

Somehow, she couldn't shake the feeling that the plane was carrying Josh out of her life forever.

The blue Pacific rolled beneath him as the 747 banked left over the Los Angeles coastline. Josh usually asked for an aisle seat to accommodate his long legs, but today he'd moved to the window. Somehow, in a flight over three-quarters full, he'd managed to score an empty seat beside him.

The sight of the bustling metropolis reduced to a collection of lighted tinker toys appealed to his melancholy mood. He felt as lost and insignificant as one of those ants piloting a pea-sized car through the dark and rapidly shrinking city.

Being in love was not all it was cracked up to be, Josh decided. Especially when the lady didn't return your feelings. Not that he could blame her. What did he really have to offer? A nomad's life, with assurances that he'd be ready to settle down in a year or two. When she'd turned down his proposal, rejection and hurt pride had brought petty, mean words from a dark place inside him. He regretted them now, with all his heart.

He sighed and turned his attention back to the window. Los Angeles was gone, replaced by the deserts of southern California. Poppy was down there somewhere. He hoped she was happier than he was at this moment.

In the past, he'd always felt a thrill of excitement as he flew out of LAX to begin a new assignment. Today, he couldn't shake the feeling that he was stuck in a grainy black-and-white movie. All the color and joy had drained out of his life when Poppy turned down his proposal. Now he was just going through the motions.

Had she received his note yet? he wondered. He'd been tempted to deliver it himself, but decided that would be selfish. Poppy had given her answer. What more was there to say? She was young, beautiful, and innocent. She'd find a man to share the life she wanted.

A man she could love with all her heart, and more important, a man worthy of her trust.

Still, he couldn't resist adding that last line. *If you change your mind, just whistle.*

Josh leaned back against the headrest. He hadn't been sleeping well lately. Maybe if he closed his eyes for a few minutes, things would look brighter when he woke up. *Right, and maybe Poppy would be sitting in the seat next to him.* He had the feeling he'd be trapped in this black-and-white movie for a long time.

"Excuse me. Mr. O'Donnell?"

Josh struggled to wakefulness. For a moment he couldn't remember where he was. Then his eyes focused and he recognized the uniform of the Aeromexico flight attendant.

He rubbed his hands over his face. "I must have fallen asleep. Where are we?" he asked.

"We're starting our descent into Mexico City. I'm sorry to wake you but I have a message for you."

Josh stared for a moment at the folded slip of paper she offered him. Who could be sending him a message 30,000 feet over Mexico?

As he reached for the paper, the flight attendant said, "I'm sorry I did not give this to you before. They called me to work for a flight attendant who is sick. I arrived late and was busy with passengers. Then you fell asleep."

Josh opened the paper. He couldn't believe his eyes.

There it was in front of him, in black and white. Suddenly the whole world sprang into vibrant color.

He turned to the flight attendant. "Did she give you this herself? A little girl with wild hair and big blue eyes?"

"Si, senor. She had wild hair and a crazy look in her eyes. For a minute, I was afraid she would try to run past security."

"I understand. Gracias. Thank you very much."

"De nada, senor." Before turning toward the rear of the cabin, she said in a soft voice, "I know what it is to be in love."

The lights of Mexico City twinkling below reminded him of the stars in the East Mojave. Stars that, at this very moment, were shining on a young lady who said she was ready to make a leap of faith.

Could he be there to catch her?

Chapter Eleven

The power to heal a troubled spirit. Poppy looked up at the opening in the rocks above her head. If ever her spirit had needed healing, it was now.

She'd risen before dawn on this Sunday morning, left Aunt El a note saying she'd be back in time for dinner, and headed for the Hole in the Wall.

The sky was a brilliant pink, shot through with streaks of orange as she descended the iron rings into Banshee Canyon. A short hike brought her to Wildhorse Canyon and the pile of boulders that marked the Indians' sacred place of rebirth.

Overhead, in the pale morning light, a mountain lion roared across the decades. Above him, bighorn sheep danced away from their human pursuers. Oddly shaped

173

symbols Poppy couldn't identify decorated the faces of the rocks.

Just looking at them gave her a feeling of peace. Hadn't these ancient artists experienced fear, love, anger, and disappointment, just as she did? They'd survived and even left a reminder of their passing for future generations.

Her gaze fell on the spot where she and Josh had huddled under a tarp during their first trek into the canyon. They felt the magic that afternoon, not only of the place but in the stirring of their hearts. If only she had trusted her feelings for Josh. If only . . .

Poppy lifted her eyes once again to the opening in the boulders. She had come here for renewal, not regrets. She began to climb.

At the top she turned in a slow circle, drinking in the wild beauty of the canyon. She loved this place. She'd always felt happiest in natural surroundings.

Poppy smiled, remembering the wild child she had been. Always wandering off someplace, frequently becoming so caught up in her explorations that she lost all track of time. Aunt El had fussed and fretted, but she and Uncle Mike seemed to understand. They'd allowed her the time and space she needed to heal. Their love and the timeless beauty of the East Mojave had accomplished what no therapist or child welfare agency could have. She'd become whole again.

Or had she? Only after she'd rejected Josh's proposal did she begin to understand how deeply her past continued to affect her. She'd been so determined not to repeat her mother's mistakes that she cut herself off from the fullness of life. She'd clung desperately to old dreams, not recognizing the chance for true happiness when Josh offered it to her.

Poppy looked out at the verdant landscape. Every scraggly little bush boasted its springtime finery. Wildflowers filled the canyon. And yet, a couple of months ago, an inexperienced traveler would surely have scoffed at the notion that so much life lay dormant in the dry desert soil.

Life, like nature, was full of change. She was ready now to embrace it. If Josh responded to her note, if he ever came back to Providence, she'd accept the love he offered, and give freely of her own. She lifted her face and arms to the canyon. "I let go of all my old fears. I'm ready to live and love with my whole heart."

Poppy felt as if a weight had been lifted from her shoulders. She stood still for a moment with her eyes closed, enjoying the warmth of the sun.

Funny, but she could have sworn she heard a whistle.

There it was again. She turned and squinted into the rising sun. In the mouth of the canyon, a small figure waved its arms wildly, a figure that looked remarkably like Josh. But that wasn't possible. Fewer than thirty-six hours ago he'd boarded a plane for Belize.

Then she heard the whistle again and saw the figure wave a hat. Even from this distance, the headgear looked battered and disreputable. Her eyes weren't playing tricks on her! By some miracle of nature, Josh O'Donnell had appeared in Wildhorse Canyon.

Poppy waved back, shouting "Josh! Josh!" She scrambled down the hill and began running across the canyon floor. Josh ran toward her. When he got close enough, she leaped into his arms.

"You came back," she gasped. He felt warm and solid, dependable, with his arms wrapped tightly around her. This was no apparition. It was the man she loved.

He bent his head to kiss her, a long, sweet, tender kiss that teetered on the edge of unrestrained passion. Poppy gave herself to it fully, willingly. Finally, he drew back, setting her feet on solid ground.

"Wild horses couldn't keep me away," he rasped. "Not even the kind with fiery red eyes."

She touched his face tenderly, still afraid to believe he was real. "I thought you were a ghost when I first saw you. How did you get back from Belize so fast?"

"I never went."

"But I was at the airport," Poppy stammered. "I gave the flight attendant a note for you."

Josh pulled a small, crumpled piece of paper from his pocket. "The flight attendant handed me this as we were flying over Mexico. She said you were most insistent about seeing me. In fact, for a minute she thought you might try to storm the checkpoint." Josh paused, his lips twitching with amusement. "I got off in Mexico

City, caught the first flight back to LAX, went home to clean up and catch a few hours' sleep, and here I am."

"But how did you find me? I didn't even tell Aunt El where I was going."

"Call it a hunch, maybe. Or intuition. I remembered how much you loved this place and the incredible afternoon we spent here. I don't pretend to understand what happened when I slipped through that knothole, but my life has never been the same."

They walked for a while in silence, each bursting with questions and explanations, neither knowing where to start. For the moment, it seemed enough just to be together, feeling the closeness they had longed for. Finally, Josh spoke.

"The note said you're ready to jump."

"I think I just did."

He stopped and faced her at the entrance to Banshee Canyon. "Tell me, Poppy. Tell me what you want. I need to hear you say it."

Poppy spoke slowly, letting the words flow from her heart. "I want you, Josh. I want to marry you, if the offer's still good. When the time is right, I want to settle down in Providence and raise a family. Until then, I'm ready to go to Belize or Tahiti or Timbuktu, as long as we're together. I've finally figured out that home isn't a place but the person you share it with. You're my home, Josh."

Josh's eyes softened to a liquid amber. "And you're

mine," he said. He took her in his arms. His kiss promised a lifetime of tenderness and passion.

She had no idea how long they clung together in the canyon. The sweetness was so intense, she felt a little dizzy. She wasn't sure she could have remained standing if Josh hadn't steadied her with his embrace. Finally he spoke.

"You know, I've been doing some thinking, too. I'm getting too old to be schlepping through swamps and rainforests for a living. I've decided to turn most of the field work over to Carlos. With the help of a few modern conveniences, like a fax machine and a good computer, I can run Outback Productions from Providence. Maybe we'll still do some traveling now and then, in the summer when the kids are out of school."

Still reeling from the effects of their kiss, Poppy wasn't sure she could trust her emotionally addled brain. She drew back to gauge the expression on his face. "Kids? Whose kids are you talking about?" she asked.

"Ours, silly. I've heard it takes at least nine months to produce one so I figure we'd better get started."

She didn't know whether to punch him or kiss him. Instead, she decided to match his teasing manner. If she was going to spend the rest of her life with this man, it wouldn't do to let him start thinking he had the upper hand. "Aren't you forgetting a small detail, Mr. O'Donnell? Like marriage?"

"I was getting to that. My offer is still good, but

there's one condition. Do you think you can manage to put a wedding together in two weeks? I still have to do the advance work in Belize and I was hoping we could make it a honeymoon."

"And if I can't?"

"Then we'll just have to elope," he said firmly. "I'm not letting you slip through my fingers again, Penelope Sullivan. So, what do you say? Will you marry me?"

Overhead, a startled barn owl took flight as the canyon reverberated with her answer. "Yes," she shouted. "Yes, yes, yes!"

Epilogue

Taken from the Providence *Herald:*

Sullivan and O'Donnell Wed
Miss Penelope Sullivan, of Providence, and Mr.
Josh O'Donnell, of Los Angeles, exchanged wed-
ding vows on Saturday, April 18, in the garden of
Poppy's Place.

The bride looked lovely in a knee-length ivory
dress of antique Irish lace. The dress was a gift
from the bride's mother, Ella Sullivan, who wore
the same gown when she married.

Miss Sullivan carried a bouquet of wildflowers
tied with a blue ribbon. A crown of desert poppies
and baby's breath decorated her hair.

The bride was given away by Homer Bell, a

friend of the family. Meg Hamilton served as matron of honor. Carlos Ruiz was the best man.

Immediately following the ceremony, guests were treated to a barbecue luncheon. The Lonely Triangle set up in the parking lot and folks danced well into the evening.

Out-of-town guests included the groom's mother and stepfather, Bridget and Mark Bellingham; his sister, Elaine O'Donnell; and nieces, Courtney, Reagan, and Katherine.

The new Mr. and Mrs. O'Donnell departed amid a shower of wild birdseed in a vintage jeep named Slim. The couple plan to honeymoon in Belize. They will make their home Providence.

Poppy set the framed clipping on her desk. The big classroom clock said 4 P.M. Where was Josh? He was supposed to pick her up early today so they could celebrate their anniversary.

So much had happened in the last five years. When Providence Elementary School opened last fall she'd been hired to teach grades K through 6. It was a demanding job but she loved it. If the area's population kept growing, the school board had promised to enlist a second teacher.

After three years of keeping company with Homer, Aunt El had finally agreed to become Mrs. Ella Bell. She'd sold half interest in Poppy's Place to Sue Mason and was content to let the younger woman handle most of the day-to-day operations. When El and Homer weren't busy with the Providence *Herald*, they enjoyed puttering around their acre and a half.

Poppy glanced at the bulletin board that covered one wall of her classroom. It bloomed with brightly colored postcards from Belize, Turkey, Thailand, Morocco, and the Cayman Islands. As Josh had promised, they'd watched the sun rise over the Sahara Desert and snorkeled off Anguilla. Her two years of globe-trotting certainly made teaching geography a lot more interesting.

She felt a tiny flutter of life and rubbed her rounded belly. The biggest change of all had taken place this winter. After five years and several visits to a fertility clinic, she'd finally become pregnant. At last, their dream of having a baby would come true. Today, on their fifth anniversary, she had a special gift for Josh.

"A penny for your thoughts."

She looked up to see her husband lounging in the doorway. "Where have you been, O'Donnell? I finished grading papers hours ago." Her smile softened the teasing words. She'd forgive the man almost anything and he knew it.

"Picking up a gift for my favorite schoolmarm." He set a small, beautifully wrapped package on the desk in front of her. "How's Sean Michael?"

The charm bracelet jingled merrily as Poppy patted her stomach. "I think he's going to be a soccer player." She picked up the package and turned it around, examining it from every angle. Finally, she put it to her ear and shook it. Her forehead puckered. "What can this be?"

Every year Josh bought her a new sterling silver charm for her bracelet and every year she pretended to be completely mystified.

He gave her the lazy smile that still made her insides quiver. "Why don't you open it and find out?"

Slowly, she undid the ribbon and lifted the lid. Inside, a tiny silver cradle was nestled in tissue paper. She felt its weight in the palm of her hand and her eyes filled with tears. "Oh, Josh, it's beautiful."

Josh came around the desk. He wiped away a tear and kissed the place where it had been. He'd been treating her like she was made of glass ever since they found out about the baby. It surprised her, but she loved his little attentions. She'd never felt more vulnerable or womanly. The life she carried inside her was so precious. She knew her rounded figure stirred Josh's protective instincts.

"Why the tears, sunshine?" He bent over her, concern etched in his face. "Are you feeling all right?"

She gave him a shaky smile. "Oh, yes. Better than all right. I've never been so happy in my life."

"In that case, I have another surprise for you."

She looked at him wonderingly. "Another surprise?"

Josh nodded. "You have to close your eyes for this one. It's out in the parking lot. And no peeking."

"Okay, but I want to take my purse."

"Why do you need your purse?"

"I'm a pregnant woman. Just humor me." She opened the bottom left-hand drawer of her desk and pulled out her handbag. Standing up beside the desk, she slung the bag over her shoulder and closed her eyes tightly. "I'm ready."

He led her down the center aisle of the school room, between rows of empty tables, to the entryway where students hung their lunch boxes and backpacks. She knew her classroom so well by now that she could have navigated it without any assistance, but Josh kept a firm grip on her arm.

"Almost there," he said.

She heard the front door open. "You certainly are being mysterious."

"Step down here. Careful." He put his arm around her and assisted her with the short step down from the modular classroom. "Okay, you can open your eyes now."

Sitting on Rover's tailgate was the most beautiful bassinet she'd ever seen. Flounces of delicate white eyelet covered the oval wicker basket. A blue ribbon curved around its rim. The front was shaded by a rounded quarter circle draped with more eyelet and topped by a blue bow. Inside, a stuffed patchwork tortoise, in shades of blue and green, peered inquisitively up at them.

Poppy couldn't help herself. She threw her arms around Josh and burst into tears.

He patted her on the back. "If you don't like it, we can take it back. It's probably too feminine. I should have waited and let you pick it out with me."

She lifted her tear-stained face. "Oh, no. It's perfect. Only . . ."

"Only what?"

"Do you think you can get another one, with a pink ribbon?"

For a moment, Josh was absolutely dumbfounded. Slowly, understanding dawned on him. "You mean, you mean, you can't mean . . ." He sat abruptly in the doorway.

Poppy sat down next to him. "Yes, darlin'. Sean Michael is going to have a sister." She opened her purse and pulled out a fuzzy black-and-white photo. "Happy anniversary, love."

With trembling fingers, Josh took the picture from her. He could distinguish two round heads. Two small bodies floated together in the surrounding darkness. "Is she sure? I mean, that it's a girl?"

"We won't know for certain until the babies are born, but Dr. Sirani has an excellent reputation for accuracy in interpreting sonograms."

"Two babies." Josh shook his head in amazement. Suddenly he became aware of the worried look on Poppy's face. He folded her in his arms and kissed her, hoping to communicate all the joy and tenderness he felt at that moment. For once, he was at a loss for words.

They clung together in the doorway of the school building, overwhelmed by the enormity of their good fortune. *I could have been happy with Poppy, even if we'd never had a child to love,* Josh thought. Now they'd have not one baby, but two. He didn't know what he'd done to deserve such a blessing but he sent up a silent prayer of thanks.

"Have you thought of a name?" he asked.

Poppy's eyes glistened with tears and her nose glowed bright pink. To Josh, she'd never looked more beautiful. "I've always liked Lauren."

Josh smiled. His wife definitely had a fondness for the stars of the silver screen. "As in Lauren Bacall. A talented lady. What about a middle name?"

"I'd like to name her for the mountains. Lauren Providence O'Donnell. It may be a little unusual, but the mountains are strong and beautiful. I know our daughter will be, too."

Josh brushed her hairline with a kiss. "Just like her mom."